GOODBYE TO THE BUTTERMILK SKY

ALSO BY JULIA OLIVER

Seventeen Times as High as the Moon

Goodbye
to the
Buttermilk
Sky

JULIA OLIVER

THE BLACK BELT PRESS
Montgomery

The Black Belt Press
P.O. Box 551
Montgomery, AL 36101

Library of Congress Cataloging-in-Publication Data
Oliver, Julia.
    Goodbye to the buttermilk sky / Julia Oliver.
        p. cm.
    ISBN 1-881320-18-9 : $18.00
    1. Title
PS3565.L477G66   1994
813'.54–dc20   94-33020
                                                              CIP

Design by Randall Williams

Manufactured in the United States of America

First Edition: September 1994

10 9 8 7 6 5 4 3 2 1

For Fairley, Julie, and Letitia
Also for my sister Chris

GOODBYE TO THE BUTTERMILK SKY

1

Summer came in quietly that year, slipped in almost unnoticed on the tail of a kind and graceful springtime. The daytime air had thickened, but the nights brought cool, sweet-smelling breezes through the window screens. Callie took that as a sign that the weather would remain gentler than usual during the hottest months. She said as much to Russell, who replied that summer in central Alabama was always the same. The rains didn't last long enough, or else real gulleywashers knocked the tender plants out of the ground and flattened the neatly spaced rows.

Still, she had the feeling that this summer would be different as she tore the May page off the 1938 calendar to reveal the one for June. If not in the weather, in some other way.

The next day Clifton Wade walked up the narrow road that wound from the highway to the Tatum house. He said later he never even saw the No Trespassing sign. His seersucker suit was wrinkled; his face gleamed with a sweat as misty as baby tears. He stopped a few yards short of the house and waited for her to notice him.

"Can I help you, Mister?" She kept on sweeping the front porch; the broom made a swishing sound, steady as heartbeats. His pale blue eyes narrowed into a squint as he lifted his face. She could see he wasn't used to hard sunshine. Her own eyes were the color of ripe scupper-

9

nongs. She could stare at the sun all day if she had to.

He said, "Ma'am, my car's about a quarter of a mile back there on the side of the road. The radiator's overheated. Could I trouble you for a bucket of water?"

"No trouble, glad to oblige. Would you like something cool to drink before you start back?"

"Thanks. That's kind of you."

"Have a seat there on the steps. I'll get you a glass of iced tea." She didn't ask him to sit in the oak swing that hung from chains attached to the porch ceiling, although he glanced at it wistfully. She closed the screen door behind her, and tiptoed down the hall to the kitchen, so as not to wake Mr. Will and the baby. Through the open door of Mr. Will's room, she could see the spiral-bladed floor fan swing in lilting rhythm, like a dancing lady, to the sounds of its own humming and his old-man snoring.

She brought the tea in a Sunday glass and sat on the top step beside him, leaving a good space between them. "Where're you from?" She surprised herself, asking that. What difference did it make where he was from? He wouldn't be from Clearwater or Deer Creek. Not that she knew every single soul in those towns, but she could tell from his clothes and the way he parted his hair and even the way he walked that he didn't come from anywhere close around.

"Birmingham."

The stretched-out syllables echoed in her mind like soft chimes. Birmingham was almost fifty miles away, over a smooth-surfaced road that had been carved through mountains, leaving exposed the rock-walled wound. She had been there twice; both times, to the state fair with her school class, once traveling by train and the other time on a bus. Her ears had popped from the altitude.

She thought it needed to be laid out there between

them before they had any more conversation. "You're married?" She made it a question, although she'd seen the gold band on his finger. He'd have noticed hers, too.

"Isn't everybody? Even you, but you appear too young to be." He looked at her then without squinting. "I'd say you're about sixteen. Seventeen at the most."

"I turned twenty not so long ago." She had felt a rounding off on that birthday and a sadness edged with fear; as if her life would be counted in decade-sized blocks of time from then on, and her next birthday would be thirty, then forty, fifty—until she was old, until she had settled into the pudding shape of her mother.

"Any children yet?" He was still looking at her, though not boldly enough to embarrass her.

"One. My baby Lucy is fifteen months old. She's inside taking a nap. So is her granddaddy, my husband's father. We live here with him. Most of the time Mr. Will sits in his wheelchair out back under a shade tree, so he can see the exact place where the edge of his land meets up with the edge of heaven." She bit her lip to stop herself from talking. She wanted to examine his face as intently as he had hers, but instead she watched some wasps building a nest in the latticework beneath the porch. She would have to remember to douse the nest with kerosene before she let Lucy play in the front yard again.

He drank the sweetened tea in long swallows and rattled the rough chunks of ice around in his glass. She had chipped up the last of a twenty-five pound block. Russell would complain about having to make another trip to the ice house. The man was contemplating the emptiness around them. "Does your husband run the farm?" Of course he could see there wasn't any activity going on out there. No tractor sounds, no little specks that were men at work in the distant fields.

She took a deep breath, wondering how much to tell him of what wasn't any of his business. "Russell works at the cloth mill in town now. The boll weevil hit our crop so bad last year he didn't make enough to pay for the fertilizer, so when he found he could get wage work, he decided to cut back this year on cotton acreage." The bare land looked like something left over from a time long past; it lay there so still she could almost hear it breathe sometimes. "That lumpy ground is where he's just plowed under a field of vetch. The government pays him something to plant a cover crop, to protect the soil in the winter, but it's nowhere near enough to get by on. It wasn't an easy thing for him to take an inside job." She didn't say it had almost killed him, or that her heart ached for him, having to go against the grain of his nature, or that her husband's unhappiness had made their marriage heavy as a rock slide, dry as a used-up creek bed. She was wishing the man beside her could have seen the field of vetch in the early spring, when it was a blanket of rich purple blooms, spread out like a blessing.

He shrugged. "Most folks I know would say it wouldn't be easy not to work inside. Matter of fact, I'd feel that way myself." He stood and smoothed his trousers down. He took a linen handkerchief from his pocket and wiped his face with it, then refolded it neatly. She saw the embroidered initial W in a corner. He said, "You have a view of the whole world's ceiling from here, seems like. Those clouds don't look like the ones I see from my office window."

She followed his gaze. "Today they're churning, like clabber." She added, shyly, "A buttermilk sky is tricky. One minute it looks like rain, the next, it's back to sunshine."

"One of nature's deceptions," he said. "It's so quiet here. Do you get lonely?"

"I stay too busy to get lonely. On the days I have a

colored girl to help out, I spend time on my sewing. That's what I like to do best. On Saturdays, after we take our eggs to market, we sometimes go to the picture show."

"So despite the boll weevil, your life is okay. You've started your family, and your father-in-law owns this comfortable house and all this land, and the hard times haven't disrupted things here as much as in some places." His voice offered reassurance in that summing up of her existence.

"What's your life like?" She told herself that would be the last question she asked him.

"My days are mostly spent in one cramped office with ten other people. We all smoke, so we can't see each other through the haze by noon. I have two children and a wife at home; I go out one night a week to bowl and another to play cards. Still I'm as lonely as if I lived in the middle of nowhere, too." He smiled like he didn't mean to hurt her feelings about where she lived. He took the last piece of ice from his glass and rubbed it across his forehead, then touched her cheek with it before putting it in his mouth. She drew in her breath; she felt as though she had pressed her lips on the same part of a cup where his had been.

"Is your wife lonely, too?" She'd broken her own rule, asked another question. She wished she could take it back. She kept her eyes on the wasp's nest.

"My wife enjoys poor health. I don't call that the same as being lonely. Thanks for the tea and the hospitality. I have to go now." He said it apologetically, as though he knew she would like for him to stay. "Could I have that water? I'll return the bucket when I come this way again in a few days."

She hurried inside, to hide her blushing and to get the water. The knowledge that she would see him again comforted her like the last resolute notes of a hymn. She prayed that the sink faucet would yield enough. If the cistern was empty, she would have to go out back and start the pump. She whispered "Thank you," wondering which one of the prayer granters was responsible—God or Jesus or some angel assigned to her—as the water gushed into the galvanized bucket. She turned off the tap when the water was within a few inches of the brim. Any more, and it would have wasted, splashed out as he walked with it.

When she returned to the porch, he said, "I promise I'll bring this back soon." She was careful not to touch his hand as he took the bucket handle from her. "By the way, my name is Clifton Wade. What's yours?"

"Caroline Tatum. Everybody calls me Callie."

He repeated it without smiling, his mouth shaping the word "Callie" like he was getting used to it.

They didn't say goodbye, and later she remembered that it became a pattern—not saying goodbye—as if they both knew that if either ever said the word, even just as a politeness, it would become the reality.

She watched him walk back the way he came, until he was hidden by the pine trees.

When Russell came in later that afternoon, anger at having been cooped up in the mill simmering like sunburn on his face, he missed the bucket right off.

She said, "I lent it to an old man who needed water for his car. He'd walked a good piece, so I told him he could drop the bucket off in a few days when he passes this way again."

That half-lie made the ones to follow easier.

By supper time, she had made herself forget the stranger's face, but not the shape of him moving toward her up the road. She watched her husband as he ate the food she had prepared, filling his mouth with it, chewing, swallowing, as though it were another chore to be gotten through. If Russell had been at home that day, not right there at the house but somewhere on the place, she would have felt his presence over her like an umbrella, and she would not have dared to look into the face of Clifton Wade, much less found out his name.

Russell said, "Why're you glaring at me like that? You mad at me?"

"I didn't mean to glare at you," she said. He should have been there to block the gaze and the path of the blue-eyed man from Birmingham.

Later that night, after Russell was asleep, she got up carefully so the bedsprings wouldn't creak and crept out to the porch. The top step where she and Clifton Wade had sat together (although with a distance between them) was warm, as though from their bodies; she could feel the pulsing heat through her nightgown. The sun was long since down, the moon had cooled things off. Still their warmth lingered and spread: her warmth toward his. She could have said his name aloud there. The crickets and tree frogs would have masked the sound of it with their own sounds. But she could savor his name on her tongue without speaking it until it was as familiar as the taste of lemon drops.

When she returned to the bed, Russell rolled over and threw an arm across her. "Baby wake up?" he asked sleepily.

"She's all right now. I patted her a bit."

"You're a good little mama, Callie." His hand found her breast and closed over it. The calluses on his fingers were like a sprinkling of gravel.

When she was sure he had gone back to sleep, she removed his hand and turned on her side, facing the window where she could see the moon just barely above the china-berry tree in the side yard. Clifton Wade would be seeing it in Birmingham, too, perched up there some-where in view despite those skyscraper buildings. That gentle moon divided the distance between them and made it seem less.

❧

Russell was four years older than Callie, and they hardly knew each other all those years they rode the same school bus into Clearwater from neighboring farms. After he graduated from high school, he went to work on the farm all day long instead of just before and after school. When she did see him, it was like she was marking time noticing him, although she didn't really have a crush on him. When she turned sixteen Russell started coming around to see her on Saturday nights; he smelled of Octagon soap and Lucky Tiger hair tonic and serious intentions. They would go into Clearwater in his pickup truck to football games or the picture show. Her daddy was pleased because people in that part of the county looked up to the Tatums. They had owned their land since the Indians, and they had more of it than most.

Russell spent three months clearing swamps over near the Georgia line for the CCC—his daddy's idea—and came back (walked away after only half the time he'd signed up for, also his daddy's idea) bragging like he'd really seen something of the outside world. She was relieved when he left, because she didn't have to worry about whether she was pleasing him or not, and glad to see him when he returned, because she had missed him terribly.

By the time she was a senior in high school none of the boys there paid her any attention because they knew she belonged to Russell. Her home economics teacher told Callie that she wanted to put her name in for a work-study program at Auburn, the state college about eighty miles away. Callie told her mama about it. It would be up to her mama to tell her daddy.

Her mama looked at her as though she'd said she wanted to join the circus. "My stars, girl, don't you want to marry Russell Tatum and have a family? What could you possibly do with college-learned home ec except teach it and end up an old maid?"

Callie waited a few days to see if her daddy would say anything to her about the college idea, but he didn't.

Russell frowned as if she'd told him someone had insulted her. "I never gave a thought to going to college myself. I figured anything I should know about farming I had already learned from my old man. I didn't want some necktie farmer telling me how to rotate crops and what all chemicals go in fertilizer. Don't look to me like you need to know any more than you already do about cooking and sewing, either." Russell had a pride about him as strong as a team of good mules. It wouldn't have let him wait four more years for her to become his wife. By the time she put on the cap and gown, she had lost all excitement about graduation; school was already in the past. She had an engagement ring on her finger, and she had made her wedding dress of white dotted swiss organdy (curtain material she'd found in the dry goods store), sewing on it after school, the time she used to spend studying.

They were married in Callie's church, the Methodist, but right away she joined the Baptist. She had to be immersed, ducked backwards by the preacher, in the bright green artificial pool by the pulpit. Faces in the choir loft looked down at her as she came up gasping. That was the first time she got mad with Russell. It was because the Tatums had always been Baptists—never had a Methodist in the family—that she'd had to go through that humiliation.

But she never stayed angry with Russell for long when they were first married. She was keyed-up happy; she took pleasure in being around him. She tried to think of ways to help him overcome his terrible shyness, which he wouldn't admit he had.

Russell and the two colored men who worked for him built a little three-room frame house on the edge of the stream that ran across one side of the Tatum farm. It wasn't finished until just before the wedding. Callie's brothers moved her hope chest and the walnut spool bed that had belonged to her grandmother in while they were on their two-day honeymoon in Montgomery.

She was glad to get back from the wedding trip. Russell was miserable in the hotel's big, quiet dining room, where the colored waiters wore gloves, because he knew that she knew he felt so out of place. His embarrassment and awkwardness almost ruined it for her, until she remembered when girls on the school bus would flirt their hardest trying to get a smile from him, and she concentrated her thoughts on how lucky she was to be married to him.

Later, Callie decided she must have got pregnant on the first night they spent in the little house, because exactly nine months and two days after they were married she had Lucy. She wanted to believe the baby wasn't started in that Montgomery hotel.

A few months after they were married, Russell's mother died suddenly. The doctor said her heart just stopped. "We got to move in with my daddy," Russell told her right after the funeral. "He can't live by himself." Mr. Will had had a stroke some years before.

"How come Lela and her family can't move in with him?" Callie asked. Russell's only sister was five years older than he was, married and living in town.

"'Cause I don't want her to," Russell said. "We'd never get her out of that house once she got back in it. It's supposed to come to me after he passes on."

"I like having our own little house. We've barely got used to it." She had just begun to fix it up.

"You'll like the big one better." Russell smiled for the first time since his mother died. "And the old man won't give you any trouble. I won't let him."

"Huh," Callie's mama said when she heard that. "Waiting on Will Tatum hand and foot is what killed his wife. You'd best get it straight with Russell right from the start what you have to do for his daddy, and not be taxed with more than you can handle." But Callie and Mr. Will got on fine. She had plenty to keep her busy, and she had the energy to do it with, even when she was pregnant. It didn't take any time to move their belongings up the hill to the big house and settle in.

Russell said, "That piece of a house was a waste of time and money. I don't know why in the world I ever thought about building it."

"It showed me you thought I was special, making us a private place to start out in," Callie said.

"Well, hell yes, I thought you were special. I proved that by marrying you, didn't I? I'll figure out something to do with the little house. Might store hay in it."

She wasn't sure whether or not he was serious. "Please don't ruin it."

He laughed. "Tell you what. We'll put our six kids in it, soon's we have 'em."

She knew he wasn't altogether kidding about six kids. A month after Lucy was born, Russell started talking about another baby, even though he was worried about making the cotton crop. Like all men, he wanted sons. According to her mama, Callie had always been her daddy's favorite, being the oldest and the only girl, but she didn't think that was so. Once he got the boys, he never paid her much attention. The main thing her daddy was proud of her for was that she had married Russell.

2

She had no idea what kind of car Clifton Wade had, but the green Nash coupe rolling up the road toward the house had to be his. It had been two days since he first came by. He would be returning the bucket.

She ran out of the house and down the steps. She didn't want Arletta or Mr. Will to see him. She told herself she would collect the bucket and turn him right around. She wouldn't even let him get out of the car.

He drove up close to where she stood and cut off the engine. The sudden silence when the motor stopped running was like the world had stopped and was waiting on them to decide something before it started up again. She raised one hand as if to shield her eyes from the sun, but she was used to the sun. She wasn't used to the brightness of him.

He said, "It's a nice day for a ride. Would you come along with me?"

"Where to?" He might as well say the moon, because she couldn't go anywhere with him.

"Deer Creek. I have business there which shouldn't take long. Afterward, we could have lunch at the Gladjoy Hotel." He got out of the car then and leaned on the door.

"How long would we be gone?"

"I promise to have you back before three o'clock. Is that soon enough?"

Russell wouldn't be home that early, but Arletta was supposed to get off at two. She said, "I'll have to make some arrangements." She left him standing there and fairly flew through the house to the kitchen.

Arletta had come in from the back yard with the clothes basket and was sprinkling the load of Russell's stiff sun-dried shirts, all made of blue cotton chambray that was woven in the mill where he worked.

"Where's Lucy?" Callie asked. Arletta had the baby outside with her while she took the wash off the line.

"You're about to step on her."

Lucy was under the kitchen table eating a graham cracker. Callie picked her up, brushed wet crumbs away from her cheek so she could find a place to kiss. "Do me a favor and stay a little later today," she said to Arletta. "Until about three? I need to go off for awhile."

Arletta sighed. "You know I have plenty of work to see about when I get home. Got to do my own wash, iron my own clothes."

Callie said, quickly, "I'll pay you an extra fifteen cents."

"Well, now," Arletta smiled broadly. "My wash can wait."

"Don't forget Mr. Will's out there and you'll have to take him to the bathroom. Else he'll wet himself."

"I know 'bout Mr. Will. Don't forget I been here longer than you."

Callie's mama said Arletta was too sassy for her own good, but Callie and Arletta understood each other. Arletta had worked for Russell's mother. After the crop failure Russell said he might have to let her go altogether, but Callie had talked him into keeping her on part-time.

People thought the Tatums, who'd always had a big spread of land and Negroes working for them in the house and fields, didn't have money problems like the other farmers in the county did. But Russell worried about money all the time. He had already taken Rafe and Willie off the payroll temporarily—Rafe was Arletta's husband—and helped them get janitorial jobs at the mill. Russell was unhappy that they knew he was only a loom operator and not anyone's boss. He kept telling Callie, reminding himself, that he was laying off planting a full crop for one year only, that working a mill shift was temporary. He said he wasn't going to be beaten by a bug no bigger than a housefly. The boll weevil had taken a toll of most of the farms in the county except Callie's daddy's, who was a dairy farmer. But the Tatums had always been cotton planters. Russell would stare out at those stripped fields, and it was like someone in the family had died.

Callie wasn't thinking about Russell or the weevil plague as she peeled Lucy's fat little arms from around her legs so she could leave. She already had on her nicest dress and her high-heeled shoes with the T-straps because she had dreamed the night before that Clifton would come back that day. She stood on a chair and checked the seams of her stockings in the mirror over the dresser. She grabbed her patent leather purse and went out the front way, right after Arletta had taken Lucy and gone out the back way.

Clifton was standing under the tree that had the tire swing. He didn't look like the kind of person who would have an old rubber tire hanging by a rope from a tree in his front yard. She had no business going off with him.

He opened the car door and held it while she got in. She sat there for an eternity while he walked around to the other side. Neither said a word until he turned onto the blacktop. Callie relaxed when they were on that smoothness; she remembered how rough and dusty it had been a few years before. Now it was like riding on silk ribbons.

"Please don't worry," he said then. "I'm a perfectly safe man."

She turned her face toward him and felt their smiles meet almost as tangibly as if their mouths had made contact. One thing that hadn't occurred to her was to worry. Not even about her hair, which was whipped about her face as the wind blew in the car windows. She had been on a few special occasions to the Gladjoy Hotel for Sunday dinner, but never on an ordinary weekday.

At first, they hardly talked at all. He sang along with music from the car radio, but she wasn't sure enough of the words to join in. He said, "This one is my favorite. It's number two on The Hit Parade," and crooned: "'Somebody else is taking my place, somebody else now shares your embrace...'" He grinned self-consciously. He knew he was the somebody else.

On the outskirts of Deer Creek, they drove past the block of warehouses and the cottonseed oil plant that smelled like peanut butter cookies baking. Once the town had been a Creek Indian settlement, a forest filled with deer. Branches of ancient oak trees reached out and touched each other, as if in remembrance of those earlier times, above the wide street that made a square around the courthouse.

Callie sat on a bench on the shady courthouse lawn while he was inside. She looked carefully to see if there were any familiar cars or trucks parked close by, ready to duck her head in case there were. The only person who glanced her way was an old colored woman sitting on the back of a mule-drawn wagon, surrounded by pasteboard crates of eggs and croker sacks stuffed with turnip greens and yellow squash. The woman called out to her in a sing-song voice, "Got some fresh yard eggs and nice tender greens today, missy."

"Sorry, I don't need any," Callie called back. She had eggs to sell of her own, and a vegetable garden that yielded just enough produce for her family, with none to go to waste.

He wasn't gone ten minutes. She wondered if he really had any business there at all. The Gladjoy Hotel, of the same red brick as the courthouse, was just across the street. As they went up the steps to the wide veranda, a parrot in a cage near the entrance squawked, "There's a pretty lady!"

It was as easy as skimming cream off the top of milk for her to pretend that Clifton was her husband. They both had on wedding rings; they were obviously married. People in the spacious, high-ceilinged room didn't seem to be paying them any particular attention. It was late for lunch-time and there weren't many diners. Clifton saw to it they were seated at an inconspicuous table behind a large wicker plant stand. They were hidden by green fern fronds that cascaded in wide arcs, like a turkey's tail feathers.

"You're to have some of everything," he said. Blue and white china dishes and tureens were passed to them by a colored woman who looked like the one on the pancake box. Callie took small portions of roast lamb with mint sauce, artichoke root pickle, spoon bread, orange halves stuffed with whipped sweet potato and raisins, butterbeans with slivers of hamhock. She wished she could tell him that she could make all those dishes and more.

Clifton hardly touched anything himself for watching her eat. She forced herself to eat more than she wanted so she wouldn't be wasting his money.

As they were leaving, the parrot called out behind her: "Come see us again, pretty lady."

Callie knew they wouldn't. Never again would she and Clifton walk into the public rooms of the Gladjoy Hotel, as though they were a normal married couple enjoying a leisurely lunch together. They couldn't take such a chance again. God had looked after her this time, seeing to it no one was there to wonder who was the man with Callie Tatum. She couldn't expect God to shield her indefinitely from curious eyes.

On the drive back, she let her thoughts drift with the radio music. There was a considerable distance between Birmingham and where she lived. He could get to Deer Creek by another route without coming near the Tatum farm. She wouldn't see him often. Maybe never again.

He laid his hand lightly over hers on the seat between them and said, "My job doesn't require me to travel this way too frequently. But if I can think up some excuse to come back this way one day next week, may I come to see you again?"

"Yes." She wished he hadn't told her the truth; she wished it would go on that he had a reason to come that way, something other than her. It was settled then, if it hadn't been before. They both sighed, with as much sadness as satisfaction, knowing what they'd agreed upon without putting words to it.

She felt as close to him at that moment, with just his hand lying on top of hers, as she ever had to Russell when he lay on top of her. She glanced at the side of Clifton's face as he watched the road. Already, his face seemed as familiar to her as her husband's. When he drove up near the house, she jumped out of the car before it had come to a full stop. He hadn't mentioned the bucket, and although she had seen it behind the seat, she didn't think to take it.

Clifton hadn't been gone five minutes before Callie heard her daddy's truck—her mama would be at the wheel— roaring and bouncing up the road. She had just given Arletta a dime and a nickel as her mama came in the front way, slamming the screen door.

"Where you been so dressed up?" Her mama looked Callie over from head to toe.

Callie was thinking it was a shame she could never introduce Clifton to her mama; she'd be so impressed with his clothes and his good looks and manners. She told the second lie. "Jane Elliot came by and took me for a ride in her folks' new car." Her mama didn't actually know Jane, a town girl who had been in Callie's high school class.

"That why you got Arletta to stay overtime?" Her mama peered through the kitchen window at Arletta, trudging homeward across the field. "Why couldn't you take the baby with you?"

"I could have, but I didn't want to. I need some time away from her occasionally." Callie looked the older woman in the eye.

Her mama looked her right back full in the eye. "So, where did you and Jane Elliot go?"

"We rode into town." Town meant Clearwater, where Callie had gone to high school and where Russell worked in the mill. It was several miles closer than Deer Creek, which was in the opposite direction. "We had fountain Cokes at the drugstore."

Her mama clucked with disapproval. "I wouldn't hang around with girls who have time on their hands and aren't married, if I was you," she said. "Russell doesn't look like he'd put up with much."

"Then let's don't tell him," Callie said.

To her surprise, her mama agreed. "I think that's wise," she said, still frowning. "But I expect you'd better watch how you spend your leisure time. If Russell thinks you have too much, he's liable to let Arletta go. And you sure need her around at least some of the time to help you with that nasty old man."

"Mr. Will's not nasty," Callie said, anxious to change the

subject even if it meant starting an argument with her mama.

"Well, he is one of God's children, and I shouldn't be un-Christian and criticize him," her mama said righteously. "But I remember the time when he was a real mess, believe you me."

"In what way?"

"I'm not going to rekindle old rumors. You can just take my word for it. He's harmless now, and a far cry from what he used to be. He was a real devil of a man. But what the Lord provideth, the Lord can take away. And He took the sap out of Will Tatum with that stroke."

"Mama, are you saying you think the Lord caused the stroke?"

"He didn't see fit to stop it, did He?"

"I guess not," Callie said. "Then why does Mr. Will pray a lot and read the Bible?"

"Doing penance," her mama said, with satisfaction. "He's trying to get through with his punishment in this lifetime so he won't have to suffer the fires of hell after he dies."

Callie changed the subject again, and soon her mama was happily telling her, step by step, as if she'd never told her before, how to put up beans so they'd keep their color and taste garden fresh even in winter.

Winter. The word hit her like a cold wind. In those gray months, would she have, as the song said, her love to keep her warm? Or just memories of it? She trembled, and a saying came quickly to her mind: Shudder for no reason, cat's walking over your grave. But she wouldn't think of winter and old age and graves. Now there was only her twentieth summer, stretched out green and golden with promise, under a blue tent of sky. Those clabber-like clouds didn't mean a thing.

∽

All that fooling around that she and Russell did once a week before they married had been a lot more exciting than what they did almost every night right after they married. When they first started going together, Russell told her if she ever let him touch her in that place he would lose all respect for her, so they parked in his truck on the creek bank for almost two years on more moonlit nights than she could remember, doing what seemed to pleasure them both without dishonoring her.

On their wedding night in the strange hotel room they were like strangers to each other. The shapes they were used to in their clothes were different out in the open. Russell was silent and determined, almost as if he had something unpleasant to get over with. After he finished, his harsh bursts of breath calmed into a long, drawn-out sigh, her blood seeped out in a small red circle of surprise onto the white sheet. Callie jumped up and wet a towel and tried to obliterate the spot.

Russell laughed. "Why, hon, I'm glad to see it. Proves I wasn't short changed on my wedding night like lots of guys are. But I knew I wasn't, anyway." He pulled her down on his lap, and she put her arms around him and held on for dear life, even when he wanted to turn loose. "Let go now, sugar," he said then. His new striped pajamas lay stiff and crumpled on the floor by the bed. His fingers shook as he took the straight pins out of them where they were folded over cardboard before he put them on, and then, as soon as they were in bed, he sat up and took the pajamas off and never put them back on. Although he was naked, he had not suggested she remove her new nightgown. When they lay down again, to sleep, she pressed up close to his smooth back, making her knees bend in to fit the angle of his, and wept a little, not knowing why; but if he was aware of it he didn't let on.

The first time her mama saw Callie alone after they got back from the honeymoon trip, she looked her over very carefully, then nodded her head, as if she had seen something she agreed with. "Sister," she said, "You're a woman and a wife now. His woman and his wife, if you get what I mean."

"You could have told me it was going to hurt," Callie said.

"It won't for long. You'll get as used to it as brushing your teeth. My advice to you is to go ahead and start your family. There's nothing sweeter than having a baby around to love."

Callie didn't know how not to start a family, so starting one was exactly what she did. After Lucy was born, the doctor told Russell that he'd better wear something so Callie wouldn't get pregnant again right away. Lucy weighed nearly nine pounds at birth and Callie had a hard time delivering her. So whenever Russell wanted to do it, he would sigh and reach in the bedside table drawer for a Trojan. But after awhile he complained. "Go back and ask that doctor if it hasn't been long enough for us to let nature take its course. Doing it with one of those things is like taking a bath with your socks on."

The second time he mentioned asking the doctor, Callie knew he meant business. "I went back to the doctor today," she said as soon as they were alone on the night after she'd been to Deer Creek with Clifton. "He told me I'd better abstain from doing it at all for awhile, even with you wearing one of those things, because I have an infection down there."

"What's he talking about, an infection?"

"He said it isn't too serious now, but it could get worse."

Callie marveled at the way she could invent and tell lies all
of a sudden when she never had before.

Russell hit the bedpost with his fist. "So we're gonna
have us some doctor bills. Did he give you any medicine?"

"No, he said the infection would clear up by itself in
time if we just didn't do it."

"Do it!" Russell said, pursing his mouth, trying to mimic
her. "You're a married woman of over two years now, and
it's time you learned to say the real words for it. The bad
words. Especially since you think 'doing it' is so bad."

"I never said it was bad."

"You never said it was good."

The conversation ended, and the time began that was a
rest for her from Russell. He was still right there beside her
in the bed every night, but he didn't roll over onto her. She
could save herself for her new love. The next time she saw
Clifton she would be empty of everything but a fierce
yearning for him that hummed inside her like music. She
wouldn't even remember what being touched by Russell
was like.

She took him at his word, that it would be a week before
he would come to see her again, and close to midmorning
on the eighth day she waited near the edge of the Tatums'
private road until she saw his car approaching. She opened
the car door and got in before he had a chance to get out
and open it for her.

He looked scared, looked younger than Russell, although she knew he was older. He said, "I'm glad you were
outside. I've been trying to figure out what I'd say if
someone besides you came to your door."

Before she lost her nerve, Callie hurriedly said what
she'd been rehearsing in her mind. "There's a little house
on the place that's vacant. Would you like to go there?" She
pointed to the remnant of an old wagon trail, with more

weeds than gravel, that angled off from the road.

"That would be wonderful. If you're sure it's okay."

She wasn't sure about anything as his car bumped slowly along the ruts toward the little house where she had begun her married life. They hid his car behind the hedgerow where it wouldn't be seen from the highway or the big house.

She took his hand and led him through the doorway. He was actually holding his breath. When they were inside, and the walls and low ceilings closed around them, he let all that breath out in a moan that alarmed her.

"What's wrong?"

"Nothing. Everything." He sat down suddenly on the couch in the living room. She leaned over him, worried that he was about to faint or something. He put his hands around her waist and pulled her close; his face rested against the round part of her stomach that never had gone back flat after she had the baby. She could feel his breath through the starched cloth of her dress.

They hardly talked at all. The time had to be spent doing what they both ached to do. But it wasn't like they were hurrying to get it over with; the pleasure came instantly and yet hovered over them teasingly, like streaky clouds over dry, cracked fields. Clifton called what they did "making love."

Afterward, with his tie re-tied and his hair combed back smooth, he looked as though he had stepped straight out of a magazine picture and stumbled, by mistake, into the small abandoned house on a big idle farm in the middle of nowhere.

He waved to her as he drove away. Something about the gesture struck her as trifling. Maybe what they had just done was unimportant as far as he was concerned. As she walked to the big house, she almost talked herself into her right mind. But by the time she reached the backyard, the sheer joy of the hour she had spent with him returned full force.

As soon as Russell came in he said, "That old fella you lent the bucket to finally returned it. I found it on the front steps."

Callie's surprise was genuine. "Is that so? Guess I was out back when he came by."

"He must have a strong sense of conscience. Plenty of people would have kept a good bucket like that."

The next afternoon, she could smell his rage the minute he entered the house. He grabbed her by both arms. "I'm on to you, Callie," he said. He was trembling with his anger.

No one could have seen her and Clifton. Not Arletta, who wouldn't have told anyway, not her nosy mama, no one.

"I called your doctor today," Russell said. "And I asked him what kind of infection was causing you to have to abstain from having relations with your hard-working husband who provides you with a home and every morsel of food that goes in your mouth, and he didn't know what the hell I was talking about."

She burst into tears.

Russell turned loose her arms and said, "Aw, quit your sniveling. The doctor explained to me why he thought you told that ridiculous story."

She stopped crying. "He did?"

"Yeah." He didn't look at her.

"Well, what did he say?" she whispered.

"He said women sometimes need a rest from it, and they make up any lies they can to get their husbands to leave them alone for awhile." Russell had a puzzled expression on his face, like a little boy who didn't know why he was being punished. "I just don't see why you couldn't have told me yourself."

Relief washed over her like cool well water. "I did need to be left alone for awhile, and I couldn't explain it to you, so I didn't try. If other women get that way too, that proves I'm normal, doesn't it? But I'm all rested up now, Russell, and if you want to do it tonight, I'll be glad to oblige you."

"Forget it. I don't care one way or the other." Russell's shoulders were drawn up in the way he kept them most of the time now that he was unhappy. After they had gone to bed that night he changed his mind. The first time of making love with Clifton made it easy for her to do her wifely duty with Russell. She kissed his shoulders and back after he had turned over on his side. When she was sure he was asleep, she got out of bed and knelt beside it to say a silent prayer, thanking God for watching over her and Clifton and not letting them get found out.

She went to sleep drained of all feeling except a peaceful acceptance of her new way of life. She really thought that God was going to protect her and Clifton from consequences too frightening to contemplate.

3

Hours and whole days skimmed by her like she was on the outside of the world watching. She and Lucy spent a lot of time in the back yard with Mr. Will. Callie had fixed a little sandbox right in his line of vision—he couldn't turn his head easily—where he could see Lucy play. Callie would be shelling peas or mending Russell's shirts or embroidering her sampler, and she would feel a tingling all over. She was buzzing inside, like she was completely in tune with crickets and frogs and blue jays that kept up a constant racket; the pulsing of pale green throats of lizards that watched from their leaf-shade was her rhythm, too.

She couldn't get it straight in her mind why she should be so happy. She had a good husband and a precious baby and they had a roof over their heads and food to eat, but she also had a problem that could burn a hole in her heart. She saw the face of the man she loved constantly in her mind, as clearly as she could see the color of the hydrangeas, the same blue as his eyes, that grew beside the back porch. She would see Clifton's happy face floating around in the limbs of the pecan tree, or his serious face still and stark on a sheet pinned to the clothesline. Then she would close her eyes and see him even better against the darkness of her eyelids.

He had been back twice since that first session of lovemaking. Each time they spent less than an hour at the little house, but it took a chunk out of her day contriving to meet him there—Arletta didn't even realize she'd left the house one of those times—and three full hours of his day driving from Birmingham and back. The last time he came, he had not told her when he would return. She would not let herself ask him.

It had been over a week since she'd seen him. She walked down to the mailbox and found a letter inside it, addressed to her, with a Birmingham postmark. Mrs. Caroline Tatum, not Mrs. Russell Tatum. She put the letter in her apron pocket where she could feel it against her thigh while she worked in the kitchen. Later that afternoon while the baby was asleep, she opened the letter, which had been written on a typewriter. Some mistakes had been penciled over, so she could see he wasn't used to typing. It wasn't long, but she skipped ahead to the ending: "Love, C." He had started off "Dearest C."

At least they had that much in common, the first letters of their given names. Clifton and Caroline; Clifton and Callie. He had told her he didn't have a nickname. Sometimes she would let herself imagine a house with window boxes full of red geraniums and a white picket fence around a yard that didn't stretch to the edge of heaven, only to other people's yards. She was trying to see herself and Clifton living in Birmingham, in a neighborhood. What he said in the letter was that everything had moved too fast for him. He couldn't even think about anything but her; he said he had thought of every possible answer to their dilemma but that it all came down to just one thing, and that was, it was simply not in the cards for them to be together. Too many people would be hurt: his wife, her husband, their children. The last line was typed in capital letters: DESTROY THIS LETTER. PLEASE FORGET AND FORGIVE ME.

Callie refolded the page inside the envelope and stuck it under the skeins of embroidery thread in her sewing basket. If the letter was all she would have to keep of Clifton, then she couldn't destroy it. She wasn't sad or angry. She was numb. Mr. Will was calling her in his strangled-sounding voice. She hurried into the kitchen where he leaned over the table, reading the Bible. He had begun to read it regularly right after he realized he wasn't going to die from the stroke that put him in the wheelchair.

"What do you need?" she asked him.

"Nothing from you, you harlot," he roared, pointing a crooked finger at her. "You're no better than the whore of Babylon."

She flinched and almost put her hands over her ears.

"Jezebel," he hissed. His eyes were wild. Fear slid over her. He couldn't have seen her with Clifton.

She made herself smile at him. "I'll bet you'd like some figs. I'll peel some for you." She turned to take a bowl from the cupboard.

"Don't touch my food with your unclean whore's hands," he shouted. "God will punish you for your wickedness!"

"Oh, be quiet, you old fool." She raised her voice to match his. She ran out of the room and left him there. After a few minutes, she looked in at him. The tirade appeared to be over. His head had drooped. A thin stream of spittle trickled from one side of his mouth, but he was breathing normally.

At least Arletta wasn't there to hear him call her those names. What if he started in on her again after Russell got home? Russell often said his daddy was crazy, and Callie would say he wasn't. Now she would have to agree with him.

The minute he came in from work she told him. "Your daddy has been carrying on something awful. He's been talking off his rocker all afternoon."

"Like how?"

"Like he's hallucinating, seeing people from the Bible," she said.

"Which people?"

"Oh, King Solomon, David the giant killer, Moses and Elijah. And—let's see, there were some more—Oh, yes, Jezebel and the whore of Babylon, whoever she was," Callie said. "He raves like he really sees them."

"Old son of a bitch." Russell laughed. "He never would go to church much when he was able bodied, except for funerals and weddings and other folks' baptisms. I'm not sure he ever got dunked himself, and he don't know a damned thing about the Bible. But I expect he knows a thing or two about whores. Maybe I ought to find him one, might perk him up a little."

"How come you have to be so crude?"

Russell flushed. "I don't mean to be," he said. "Not around you, Callie. Least I should do is give you the respect due a lady in my talk, and I will make a better effort to from now on. And if he rails on any more about whores around you, whether they're in the Bible or not, you let me know and I'll put him in the old folks' home."

"It's all right, Russell. I can overlook it, at least for awhile. He's just a little bit crazy now. We don't have to put him away unless it gets a whole lot worse." She meant that. She had always liked Mr. Will. And he wasn't living in their house, they were living in his; it wouldn't be right to put him out of his own place.

After Russell had gone into the old man's room to get him sponge-bathed and into his pajamas for bed, she heard them both laughing like normal. Later, as Russell was about to crawl into bed beside her, Mr. Will shouted out— they heard it over the open transom, and through the

walls, loud as thunder or a revival preacher—"Don't you
defile your body with that harlot, son!" Russell stared at
her. "Damn it," he said. "What's eating that old buzzard,
anyway?"

∾

"Don't you touch my food, girl. I mean it." Mr. Will was in
his wheelchair at the kitchen table. Callie had placed a
steaming plate of hotcakes in front of Russell and was
coming out of the kitchen with one for the old man. Russell
had his mouth open for the first bite; it stayed open in
surprise.

The old man repeated it. "I don't want you, Callie, to
touch my food ever again." He didn't sound enraged as he
had the day before. He spoke quietly and calmly. His hands
were still folded; minutes before, he had asked the blessing.

Russell leaned across the table. He, too, spoke quietly
and calmly. "Now just what the hell do you mean, you don't
want my wife to touch your food? Since when does she not
do the best job in the world taking care of you? What you
got against Callie all of a sudden, Daddy?"

The old man drew his skinny shoulders up as though he
wanted to hide his head with them. "I made up my mind,
son, so you needn't try to talk me out of it. I ain't going to
eat any food that has been prepared by a harlot."

Callie laughed from sheer nervousness. Lucy jumped
up and down and laughed too. Mr. Will suddenly grinned
and beamed as though he had told a wonderful joke.

Russell looked from one to the other. He began to
laugh himself, at first uneasily, then wholeheartedly, until
tears squeezed out of the corners of his eyes. "He thinks
you're one of those bad women in the Bible, Callie," he
said. "He's got us mixed up with those wild stories in the

Old Testament." He finished the rest of his breakfast in great mouthfuls, still chuckling. Callie set the plate she'd intended for Mr. Will on the table in front of him and busied herself feeding Lucy. Russell wiped his face with his napkin, stood up, gave the baby a kiss and then kissed Callie, which he never did in front of anybody, even his daddy. "Try to ignore this situation, hon, until I figure out what to do about him." He gave her a pleading look as she handed him his lunch pail.

She heard the noise of the truck starting up, the chickens squawking like they'd never heard it before, like they always did. The old man stared down at his untouched food. She took his knife and fork and cut the hotcakes into small squares, then poured cane syrup over the pieces until they were soggy enough for him to swallow without a lot of chewing. She held a forkful toward him and said calmly, "I'm not going to forgive you for calling me those names until you tell me why you did it."

"There ain't no two ways about it. The Bible makes it clear enough. Any woman who goes to bed with a man other'n her lawful husband is a whore and a harlot and there is no forgiveness for her on God's earth." Bits of food sputtered out of his mouth around the words.

Callie put the fork down. She stood and took Lucy from her high chair. He could feed himself or starve; why should she care? "I am not a harlot and you know it," she said.

"Then how come you go off with men who ain't your husband?"

"You haven't seen me go off with any men."

"Well, Arletta saw it," he said, slyly.

Arletta was coming in the back door. She looped the handles of her large purse on the hall hat rack as she took an apron from it. Then she came into the kitchen and took Lucy from Callie. "What is it I saw?"

"Mr. Will says you've seen me going off with men,"
Callie said. "Did you tell him anything like that?" She put
her hands on her hips and glared from one to the other of
them, like her mama did when she wanted to remind her
brothers who had the upper hand.

Arletta rolled her eyes. "Sugar, I ain't told him nothing.
He makes up things in his mind is all. Lots of old folks do
that. Then they think what they made up is the truth."

Callie wanted to shake the old man who was eating the
food she'd prepared for him as though nothing else was on
his mind. "You hear that? Arletta says she didn't tell you
any such thing. Now, I mean for you to get this notion out
of your head, Mr. Will."

He said, his voice wavering, "Well, if I didn't see you
going off with those men myself, somebody must have told
me. Maybe it was the angel of the Lord, same as told the
prophets in olden days the terrible secrets."

Callie said, "I don't imagine the angel of the Lord would
pick you to be a prophet. My mama, and my husband your
son, both said you never took to your religious ways until
you had that stroke. Before that, they said, you were a
mess." She wiped his mouth firmly with his napkin and
pushed his wheelchair into the front room. He played
checkers by himself in there sometimes in the mornings;
he liked to play both sides. Russell said that was so he could
be sure to win, but it was also because nobody took the
time to play with him. Callie thought, as she shoved him up
to the card table and put the checkerboard out where he
could reach it, that he really wasn't much trouble. He was
just another fixture that required regular maintenance. He
was so quiet most of the time he well might have begun
living in his imagination.

When she went back to the kitchen, Arletta was standing by the sink shaking her head from side to side. "He a

sight today, ain't he?" she said gleefully.

For the rest of the morning, Callie was aware of Arletta's glances as they cooked down figs with lemon peel and sugar in the big boiler, then packed and sealed the thickened preserves in pint jars. They could work together as smoothly as a matched team pulling a wagon, and usually they didn't have to talk much to understand each other's ways. But that morning Arletta watched Callie as if she were trying to read something from her face. Finally, she said, casually enough, "Have you got yourself another man, Miss Callie?"

"No." Tears slid down her cheeks.

"Hush now, honey," Arletta said. "Don't let that old man's crazy talk make you sad."

"That's not what's making me sad. I'm crying because I did have someone, but now he has ended it, and I didn't want it to stop. I can't forget him even though he's told me I have to."

Arletta's sigh was like wind moving through trees that were a thousand years old. "You mustn't tell nobody else what you told me. Now we both got to keep the secret, and I reckon I don't need to know any more about it."

At least some of the world lifted from her shoulders after she confided that much in Arletta. They got the jars filled, topped with rubber rings and brass lids, and lined up on the kitchen table without any more conversation. Right after they'd finished, Callie's mama came in, yoo-hooing her way from the front to the back of the house.

"Well, if that isn't a pretty sight," she said, admiring the row of jars. "I certainly did train you right, Sister. You're as good a cook as I am."

"It was Arletta's idea to put the lemon rind in," Callie said. Her mama didn't have a colored girl to help her out, so she tended to ignore Arletta.

They heard him yell out then, straining his vocal cords, "Who's making that goddawful racket in there?"

Callie's mama marched into the living room and said, "Now, you listen to me, Will Tatum. Just because you're not able-bodied like you used to be doesn't mean that everyone has to pussyfoot around you. And I don't appreciate you swearing around my daughter; I didn't raise her to be shouted at, either." She was puffing like a pouter pigeon.

The old man quieted down some as he said, "I'm the one who owns this place and I sure as hell don't have to put up with having a whore in my kitchen."

"Oh, shut your mouth!" Callie's mama protested in her shock-and-outrage voice. "There is no more respectable colored girl in this county than Arletta. She is certainly not that word you called her." She turned to Arletta, who was observing from the kitchen doorway. "Don't you pay him one whit of mind, girl. He's plumb crazy. The combination of his old fast-living ways, including the drinking of rotgut moonshine whiskey and I won't say what all else, plus that stroke that the good Lord dealt him, has pickled his brain altogether. Here, girl. I want you to have this." She held out a nickel as though it were a pearl.

Arletta mumbled something under her breath that Callie knew wasn't anything like a "thank you" and took the nickel.

4

Dear C:

You didn't say in your letter whether I should answer it, but since you didn't say for me not to, I am taking the liberty of writing this to your business address which was on the envelope. I agree with what you wrote, and I know you are absolutely right to say that you cannot come here again to see me. I want to make it very clear to you that all that happened was of grave importance to me. I will never forget the little bit of time we had together, and I will think of you often, maybe even when I am an old lady. I wish you would send me a picture of yourself but I will understand if you don't want to. This may seem funny, but I wish you could tell your wife and children hello from me—I feel as if I know them, just from knowing you for a little while. Good luck to you, and always count me as one of your friends.

Sincerely,

C.

She wrote the letter out three times in pencil on a lined tablet, each version a little different, before she copied the last one in ink on pink ragged-edge stationery that her aunt had given her for a graduation present. A week had passed since she got the letter from Clifton. She had used the last stamp for a Sears Roebuck order the week before, so she put the envelope with her letter inside in her purse, not sure how she would mail it. She took his letter out of the sewing basket and read it again to be sure hers fit in with it. She wanted it to sound like they were having a face-to-face conversation.

She thought about calling her mama on the phone and asking her if she would drive her and Lucy into town. Her mama could be counted on to take Lucy for a cherry smash; while they were in the drugstore, Callie could go up the street to the post office. But Miss Jessie, the postmistress, wasn't bashful with her curiosity. After she sold Callie the stamp, she would look at the address on the letter and say something like, "I declare, I didn't realize y'all had kinfolks in Birmingham." Callie decided the best way to send it would be to put the letter, with three pennies for a stamp right beside it, in the mailbox down at the roadside.

She checked on Mr. Will. Since the day before, when he had called her the names, he had been his usual mostly silent self. Before he left for work that morning, Russell fed his daddy breakfast and wheeled him down the ramp to his place under the tree. That was Russell's way of letting her know that he felt bad about his daddy turning on her.

"Ring your bell if you need me," she said to Mr. Will. He smiled at her as though he had no quarrel with her at all. She didn't tell him she was going to the mailbox. The postman usually came before noon. He'd drop her letter into his bag with a bunch of other mail where it would not be attributed to her by anyone at the post office.

She was running lightly, bouncing Lucy against one hip. When she was almost to the end of the road she raised her eyes and got such a shock she almost let the baby fall. Clifton's car was parked on the side of the highway near the mailbox. Lucy pointed her finger and said, "Man, man."

In his sharkskin suit and polka dot bowtie, he reminded

Callie of the life-sized cardboard display in the men's wear section of Goldman's Dry Goods Store. His shoes glowed with a buffed wax finish. She felt the dust of the road inside her own sandals. She was glad she hadn't begun the housework, which would have started her sweating. ("Women perspire," her mama would correct her. "Men and mules sweat.")

She took the letter she'd written from her purse. He was probably thinking she looked silly walking to her own mailbox in her house dress and apron with her Sunday pocketbook over one arm. "I was going to leave this in the box for the postman to pick up." She handed it to him. At least she had saved three cents of Russell's money.

Clifton took the envelope, folded it and stuffed it inside his shirt pocket behind a matching clip-on fountain pen and mechanical pencil. She had felt those little hard things against her breast the first time he kissed her. Most of the other times, he didn't have a shirt on.

"I'll read it later," he said. "I'm sorry about my letter. I shouldn't have mailed it. What I wrote was true, but it didn't mean anything to me." He reached out and caressed her cheek lightly with one finger, and then he did the same to Lucy. "She's a pretty little girl. Looks like you."

"I guess she does. She doesn't favor Russell at all."

He nodded as though they had agreed on something important. "Let's take a ride." She hesitated, and he said, "Please. Just for a few minutes."

Lucy sat in her lap while they rode. The preacher could have seen them at that moment and Callie wouldn't have felt the least bit ashamed, because she had a family feeling about them: herself, Clifton, and Lucy. She didn't know where that left Russell and Mr. Will and her own folks. What seemed right was the three of them driving in that car like they had someplace to go. Clifton drove slowly up and down the highway, using side roads to change direction. Once, in a secluded turn-round spot, he let the motor idle and leaned across Lucy's head and kissed Callie briefly on the mouth. She tasted the sting of concentrated mouth-wash drops on his tongue and was touched; he wanted not to smell of tobacco around her. He didn't know that all the men in her life—her daddy, her brothers, her husband, Mr. Will—customarily smelled of tobacco without seeing any reason to do something about it. Every morning and every night, Russell stuck a cigarette between his daddy's lips and patiently waited while the old man took a few labored drags from it.

She remembered that Mr. Will was out in the back yard by himself, with no one else on the place—it wasn't one of Arletta's days—and she told Clifton she had to go home. They had hardly talked at all during that aimless ride. Lucy had filled the silence with her mostly incomprehensible baby talk.

"I could come back tomorrow. Will your colored girl be there?" His hand brushed her knee as he shifted gears.

"Yes." Her knee burned from his touch.

"Then meet me at your little house. I'll hide the car like we did before. Is ten o'clock too early?"

Callie had gotten out of the car with Lucy, who squirmed to get back in. "Ten's fine," Callie said, as she jerked Lucy away from the car. Lucy went limp in her arms and howled all the way to the house. By the time she reached the front porch Callie heard Mr. Will calling, "Help me, somebody please help me." She hurried around the house to the back yard. He lay beside the wheelchair on the ground. A thin red line of blood traveled from his chin down his shirt front, but she could see the cut wasn't deep. She put Lucy in her sandbox and knelt beside Mr. Will.

"How come you tried to get out of your chair? You

knew I would be back to get you." He whimpered like a baby. She heaved him into the wheelchair, put Lucy in his lap, and rolled the chair up the ramp into the house. By the time Russell came in from work, she had Mr. Will and Lucy so clean the whole place smelled like soap.

"I was inside, but I heard him call out, so I got to him right after he fell," she told Russell. She almost believed it herself.

Mr. Will didn't answer when Russell asked him why he tried to get out of his chair, but he hadn't lost his voice. When Russell asked him to say the blessing over supper, the old man said he was through praying because it didn't do any good. So Russell said the blessing, and after he said "Amen," Lucy clapped her hands and squealed: "Man, man, man! Car, car, car! Kiss,kiss, kiss!"

"Well, listen to my baby girl. She's just learning to talk up a storm." Russell grinned and began to eat.

Lucy chanted, "Kiss, kiss, kiss. Mama kiss."

Russell's attention was on fried okra, boiled ham, and biscuits spread with fig preserves. He said, "My little girl's mama is a mighty good cook."

∼

Callie spent half an hour bathing and getting ready. She smoothed Hinds Honey and Almond lotion all over, not just on her hands as she usually did, and put on a striped chambray skirt and blouse that she'd sewn up back in the spring, a long time ago, before Clifton.

"Don't your mama look sassy, Lucy? Smells sweet, too," Arletta said when Callie finally came out.

Callie wondered if she'd overdone the lotion. She wouldn't want to attract bees. "I'm not dressed up anything special," she said. She headed toward the front door. She didn't want Mr. Will to see her leave. She had rolled him out and left him in the usual spot, this time tied to the wheelchair with a bathrobe sash. Callie had reassured herself that he couldn't see the little house through the crape myrtle Miss Ruth, Russell's mama, had planted years before from little shoots somebody gave her. Miss Ruth had nurtured that hedge until she died. Now it was a good ten feet high, its branches trained from years of pruning into a dense wall of foliage. By late July the bushes would be heavy with pink blooms that looked like wads of cotton candy.

"We gonna start on the beans today?" Arletta asked, still eyeing Callie with interest.

"We might get to them later. Right now I'm on my way to check on things around the other house. I expect I'll be there a good while," Callie said. Arletta nodded, pleased. With Callie gone, she would watch Lucy play in the sandpile and Mr. Will sit and vegetate, while she rested herself for a spell in the glider swing.

Callie had to slip away from Lucy. Once out the door she walked quickly to the meadow that ran between the big house and the little one. Russell hadn't mowed in the last few weeks—he was waiting until better hay time—so she took a footpath where the grass wasn't waist high and full of surprises such as lizards and rats and snakes. From a hundred yards away, she could see the back end of Clifton's car, rounded like the rump of a pony. He was sitting on the foot-high porch of the little house with his coat off and his tie loosened. He stood when she approached.

She didn't want to spoil the first few minutes of getting used to him again with idle talk, but as usual she said the first thing that came to her mind. "This trail is awfully rough for a nice car like yours."

"I don't mind rough, as long as it's not dangerous. I do feel nervous when I turn off onto your private road. I can't help but wonder if your husband's posted some snipers to shoot trespassers." Callie wished he hadn't said that, even jokingly. He did the same thing he'd done the day before; he reached out and touched her cheek. "I like your little girl, but I'm glad you didn't bring her this time."

He had already raised windows in the front room. Callie watched dust motes swirl in a shaft of sunlight and was embarrassed at the curtains that hung limp as old dishtowels and the hot, musty smell that was like the inside of a cotton gin.

Clifton was unbuttoning her blouse, murmuring that he couldn't get the thought of her out of his mind, and she was wondering why it hadn't occurred to her before to get the place cleaned up for him. He had spread a pallet on the floor—something he had brought with him, she knew he hadn't found it there—in a corner of the front room. The other times, they had lain on the couch; the broken springs in the seat clanged like church bells.

"Maybe the floor won't be too hard. At least it won't set up a racket," he said. The whole time he held her and touched her and said things to her, he looked beyond her, out the window to the road, and she looked over his shoulder through the open doorway toward the big house. They had to be on guard, he said. Callie didn't mind the fact that they couldn't look into each other's eyes while they clung to each other. That would be like drowning.

She felt like she had put up a bushel of beans by herself after that half hour of lovemaking. But the beans were still waiting. "I have to get back now," she said, as she began to button her blouse and tuck it inside the waistband of her gathered skirt.

"Not yet," Clifton said. He pulled her blouse loose and started over.

"I didn't know you could do that," she said.

"Do what?" He was breathing hard again.

"Do everything all over right away," she explained.

"I didn't know myself 'til now," he said.

The next time she looked at his wristwatch, another half hour had gone by. Clifton sat up. He held his head in his hands and shuddered.

"What's wrong?" She felt helpless like she did with Russell when he was in a real feel-sorry-for-himself mood.

"Everything," Clifton said. "Except you, and the fact that we're together."

A slow, easy rain had started. "I have to go now," she said again.

He raised his face and caught her wrists with his hands. "We'll get married, Callie," he said. "It's going to take awhile, there's a lot to work out, but we have to. I'm not going to let you stay with another man."

"I'm joined to him until death do us part." She felt silly saying words that seemed so weightless.

"We both made serious mistakes marrying the people we did."

She heard that pronouncement as though it had been spoken by an actor on the picture show screen. "You think so?"

"I know so."

She didn't want him to say any more then. He'd given her enough to think about. She left without touching him again, without looking back. She ran, not caring whether she had found the path, through the calm and steady rain. The light stinging way it beat upon her reminded her of the few times her mama had switched her. Her clothes were already crumpled; it wouldn't matter if they got soaked. She stopped about halfway to the big house and watched until she saw the flash of color that was his car moving through the trees and brush toward the highway.

Arletta was serving mashed-up black-eyed peas and corn bread to Mr. Will. Lucy was in her high chair feeding herself Jello, but mostly throwing it around. None of them looked up as Callie crept by the open door to the kitchen. She took off her wet clothes, put on her wrapper and lay down on the bed that she and Russell slept on together. What would happen to the bed if she went away? Could she take it, since it was hers to begin with, or did the bed now belong to Russell? Could she take their child?

In the next room, Arletta hummed a lullaby as she put Lucy down for her nap. Callie got up. She wanted to snatch Lucy out of her crib and hold her tight, but she saw from the doorway that Lucy was almost asleep, curled up with her thumb in her mouth.

Arletta came out and said softly, "You just looking for trouble." She didn't mean trouble like waking up the baby.

"I can't help it," Callie said.

"Well, I ain't judging you."

"Thank you for that," Callie said.

"I ain't judging you, but I'm warning you, Miss Callie. You are going to get caught if you don't stop. And a man like Mr. Russell would kill a man he thought was messing around with his wife."

Callie closed her eyes and tried to wish Arletta's words out of the air.

5

Russell's sister Lela hardly ever put in an appearance at the farm. Russell said it was because she felt guilty about not keeping her daddy part of the time. Callie knew Mr. Will didn't want to stay in town in Lela's row house in the mill village anyway. ("Have to live close as niggers," he'd said once after spending a week-end there. "Look out a window, see into somebody else's ten feet away.") Two days after Callie had last seen Clifton, Lela paid a surprise visit. She settled herself in the center of the porch swing with a glass of iced tea and a plate of oatmeal cookies that Callie brought her, then said, "Russell told Jerry that Daddy's been acting peculiar." Lela's husband Jerry was a supervisor at the mill where Russell worked.

"He did carry on for a couple of days about people in the Bible, but I think he's over that now." Callie spoke softly, so Mr. Will wouldn't hear them talking about him. He was inside, listening to his favorite program, "Ma Perkins," on the Philco.

Lela sighed. "Do you think it's time to put him in the old folks' home in Deer Creek?"

It would certainly make things simpler for her if he weren't around. But things would never be simple for her again, anyway. "No," she said. "He belongs here."

"I'm glad to hear you say that. Lord, he'd die if he had to leave this farm. I thought it was working out fine when

Russell was here most of the time and could be responsible for his own daddy, but it's not right for you to be saddled with him all day long the way it's been since Russell went to work at the mill."

Lela never missed a chance to criticize Russell. Callie said, "Russell helps out all he can. He still bathes his daddy and gets him in and out of bed."

"You're lucky you have Arletta some of the time, too. Last one I had was so sorry I let her go."

Arletta was feather-dusting in the front hall and over-heard that remark. Later, after Lela had gone, she said, "Couldn't pay me to work for a white woman like Miss Lela. Her mama was a good lady, but that one is plain ornery."

Callie walked with Lela to her Dodge. Suddenly, she envied her sister-in-law that automobile. If she had a car, Clifton wouldn't always have to come to her. She could drive to Birmingham, or they could meet some place halfway between. She was so busy daydreaming she was caught off guard by Lela's sly question. "Callie, what were you doing in the Gladjoy Hotel the other day, having lunch with a handsome stranger?" Lela looked like she'd just won the blue ribbon for the best pie.

"Who says I was?" Callie kept her gaze level with Lela's and did not let her eyes even blink.

"I'm not at liberty to say. But that someone said you were laughing and leaning across the table to flirt with the man."

"Well, I wish that person would say how I'm supposed to get away from taking care of my baby and your daddy and running this house to go off and have myself a fling."

Lela studied her face for a few seconds. "I made that point when she told me. I certainly want to protect the family name against slander."

Callie said, "I have a right to know who's saying these things about me."

Lela looked at her intently for several seconds. "Well, here's how it was. Jenny Hagood and I were in the hardware store, and as we came out, a man and a woman who looked like you came down the front steps of the Gladjoy Hotel and got in a green coupe with what Jenny says was a Birmingham license plate. I've been brooding over it ever since. I didn't even tell Jerry. I could hardly bring myself to confront you today, but I decided I had to."

Callie let her breath out slowly. "You're mistaken. Your eyes must have played a trick on you." She stared at Lela again without flinching, and finally Lela's gaze wavered.

"You swear, Callie? On a Bible?"

"If it means that much to you, I'll go inside and get the Bible and swear on it," Callie said.

Lela laughed uneasily. "If I'd really been convinced it was you, I'd have come out here that very day and accused you face to face. I was busy buying something, and Jenny thought she saw you through the store window. By the time we got out to the street the car had pulled off and we couldn't tell who was in it. I cussed her out for even thinking it was you in that car, much less having the audacity to tell me that my own sister-in-law was off flitting around with a strange man."

"But Jenny couldn't see inside the hotel from across the square, could she?"

Lela blushed. "I made that part up. We figured they had been in the dining room, since it was lunchtime. If I was going to sneak off with some man, I'd certainly flirt with him." She gave Callie a playful slap on the arm. "I never for one minute thought it was you. I was just having fun teasing you."

Later, as Arletta vented her steam about Lela, Callie

wondered whether what she'd told Russell's sister counted as another lie.

∾

When she awoke on Saturday morning, the sky was rose-tinged with sunrise. Russell was already out on his big red McCormick, steering from its high seat as the tractor waded into the ocean of pale green Johnson grass. He said cutting the hayfield relaxed him. He liked to watch the tall sword-like stalks fall before the sickle bar. She saw him from the window by her bed as if he were in a framed picture. Naked to the waist, ruddy from years of working in the fields without a shirt on his back (the color never really faded from one summer to the next), he reminded her of an Indian chief. It was said that one of the early Tatums had married a Creek tribeswoman. Callie had been impressed with the legend that he was one-eighth Indian, but Russell didn't want to acknowledge any "tainted" blood.

She dressed quickly and went to wake Lucy. They would gather eggs together, a ritual the child liked and did not yet realize was a chore. Lucy had learned how to ease an egg down into the basket without putting even a hairline crack in the shell.

The clatter of the mowing machine sounded as though they were really farming again, although they weren't. The night before Russell had told her that his small piece of a cotton crop was laid by; there was nothing else to do until picking time, and there wouldn't be much to pick. Now, well into July, it was apparent the boll weevils had had a second hatch-out despite the applications of poison dust. The plants were scantily clad with the pretty blooms that would make the bolls. If a cotton field didn't look like a flower garden by the fourth of July, then it could be considered a failure. "It proves I was right not to plant the whole place," he said, with gloomy satisfaction.

Rafe, hired for the day, was at the back door. "Miss Callie, I found this on the porch of the little house. Look like somebody's wallet." He held it out to her.

She didn't dare look closely at the thing with the colored man watching her. Flustered, she said as though scolding him, "What were you doing down there?"

"Mr. Russell asked me to go check around the place, be sure nobody camping out there. I saw that thing right near the door. So I brung it here to you."

Callie could hardly wait to get to the bedroom and close the door and look inside Clifton's wallet. Touching the smooth leather made her think of touching him. She found pictures of his family encased in cellophane. His wife was vaguely pretty, older than she was, maybe his age. She discovered new things about him from his driver's license. His whole name was Clifton Augustus Wade, Jr., and he lived at 1254 Maple Avenue in Birmingham, Alabama. She already knew he was thirty-two years old. Now she learned that he was five feet ten inches tall, weighed one hundred and fifty pounds. Russell was twenty-four years old, six feet one, a hundred and sixty pounds. She thought she shouldn't be looking at Clifton's personal things, but she couldn't help it. She pulled open every flap and examined cards, printed with his name and business address and the telephone number; three torn stubs of Ringling Brothers Circus tickets and two fragments of Alabama Theater tickets. That was where a man played the organ during the picture show intermission and the audience was supposed to sing along, following the ping-pong ball as it bounced over words flashed on the screen. Jealousy tore into her. He had been to those places without her.

There was another, more brittle Kodak print of his wife,

tucked away in an inside place where he wouldn't see it every time he opened the wallet, and she was younger—probably about Callie's own age. And very pretty, then. Somehow she wasn't jealous of that snapshot. She didn't touch the green bills neatly placed in the long pocket, and she was sure Rafe hadn't, either. Rafe! She had snatched the thing from him without any explanation. She took a dime from her purse and went back out and gave it to him. "I'll find out whose wallet this is," she said. "There's no reason to worry Mr. Russell with it; he has enough on his mind. So please don't say anything about finding it at the little house. Understand?"

Rafe looked at the shiny coin she'd placed in his palm, and then he looked her clear in the eye, something he had never done before. He said solemnly, "No'm, I won't say nothing to Mr. Russell. Nothing a-tall."

The whole thing with Clifton was getting out of hand. There were too many coincidences and close calls. And yet she still was aware of some protective presence; she honestly thought some celestial being—her guardian angel or Jesus—was watching over her, over them. She hid the wallet in her sewing basket and went to the telephone.

"Number please?" Edna Purvis, the operator, always recognized everyone's voice.

Callie would try to sound different. She enunciated carefully: "I'd like to make a call to this number, station to station, in Birmingham." She read the number off from Clifton's business card.

"You don't sound quite like yourself, Callie," Edna said. "You got a cold?"

"Sort of," Callie said, giving up the fake Yankee accent. She heard the number ring several times.

Finally, Edna said, "Looks like you'll have to call again later. Want me to try it for you and ring you when I get it?"

"Oh, no. It's not that important. I'll try it sometime later myself."

"Since when is a long distance call all the way to Birmingham not important?" Edna said, but Callie hung up as though she hadn't heard her. Clifton's office was probably closed, since it was Saturday. She wouldn't dare ask Edna to look up his home phone number, even if she dared call him at home.

Russell had come in for lunch when the phone rang two short rings, their signal on the party line. She heard him pick it up and say, "Call to Birmingham? You sure about that, Edna? Okay, I'll tell her."

Callie ran into the bathroom, locked the door and flushed the toilet to make some noise, which was all she could think of to do to gain time. Russell was standing in the bedroom door with his arms folded across his chest when she came out.

"Your party still doesn't answer," he said.

"What party?" She walked past him.

"Your call to Birmingham. You tell me what party."

"Oh, for heaven's sake. I told Edna not to bother trying that number again. I was calling a piece goods store that's supposed to have a big selection at good prices. I need to make Lucy and me both some clothes." She heard herself like she was someone else talking.

"One thing I don't need is for you to run up a long-distance telephone bill. Now I plain won't have that, Callie. You'll just have to mail your orders in instead of calling." Russell pounded the door jamb with his fist, driving the point home about who was boss in the house. He was also venting his anxiety. He wanted to believe her story about calling a store, because he didn't know anyone in Birmingham to call on the telephone, so how, possibly, could she? He said, "Did I make myself clear?"

"Yes," she said.

"Good." He put his arms around her and kissed her heavily. The skim of dusty sweat that had dried on him gave off an odor as familiar to her as the scent of honeysuckle on the pasture fence or hot, wet feathers on a chicken being plucked. She was so used to it she didn't think about it one way or the other. She felt the stiff hair on his chest through her dress.

He shut the door to the hall and started to loosen his belt. He was going to do it with his dirt-caked shoes and rolled-down socks on. Clifton's socks stayed smooth over his calves with garters, and sometimes, before he made love to her, he would take them off and lay them neatly aside with his other clothes. When Russell decided on the spur of the moment—on Saturday or Sunday afternoon—that he wanted to do it, he never took off anything but his pants, and sometimes not even those.

Five minutes later, he had flopped off of her onto the chenille bedspread. She lay there for a few seconds, then got up. As she stood, she felt a wetness sliding down her legs. She stared at Russell. "You didn't wear anything!"

"Well, I sure as hell didn't. The doctor said it's okay now for you to get p.g. again." Callie had never heard a man say "pregnant." The word must have been invented for women only. If they had to acknowledge the condition, men abbreviated it with initials, or called it "expecting."

She went into the bathroom, locked the door, and started running water into the tub. Her anguish was so acute she felt it as physical pain. Clifton wouldn't want her if she had another baby by Russell. She sat on the side of the tub, taking her clothes off, frantic to wash Russell's baby-making stuff away. She felt as though she might vomit.

The morning sickness! That was it. She was queasy in

the same way she had been when she was early-on pregnant with Lucy. She had assured Clifton during that first lovemaking session that it was her safe time of month, and she had thought it more or less was. (But she'd heard Lela say once there was no such thing as a safe time, just some times were safer than others.) Even her breasts began, at that moment, to feel heavier. She held them in her hands as she crouched in the tub. As the warm force of water from the faucet washed Russell's mess away, she felt a rush of pleasure like she had with Clifton.

She came out of the bathroom with the towel around her. Russell got off the bed, fastened his pants, grinned at her and said, "Now you ought to thank me for that little quickie, honey. You look more relaxed than you have in a long time."

6

Mr. Will looked like a doll they had dressed up in a suit and starched shirt and necktie. He peeped from under the brim of his ancient Stetson felt hat with darting, suspicious eyes as Russell hauled him, like a sack of potatoes, from the car up to Callie's mama's front porch. They were visiting her folks for Sunday dinner. The service at the Baptist Church let out half an hour later than the Methodists', so by the time they arrived her mama was well into preparations. Callie left Lucy showing off like a little monkey on the porch with her brothers, her daddy, and the Methodist preacher and his wife.

"Nice of the preacher's wife to come in here and lend a hand," Callie said as she mixed slivered cabbage and carrots with mayonnaise. Her mama didn't like cole slaw made too far ahead.

"That's not very Christian of you," her mama said. "That poor woman probably works harder in the parsonage than you and I do in our houses, with people coming there to see him all through the week. She deserves one day of rest."

"She doesn't deserve a day of rest any more than you do, Mama," Callie said. "You're going to drop one of these days, if you don't stop doing for everybody else. All this troublesome dinner. It's not Christmas or Thanksgiving, it's just an ordinary Sunday."

The chicken pieces sputtered and hissed in the black iron skillet. Callie was glad they weren't having frog legs, which always jumped in the frying pan as though they were still attached to live frogs. Her mama held one flour-coated hand well away from her Sunday dress, which wasn't fully protected by her apron. With her other hand she turned the drumsticks, thighs, and breasts in the deep bubbling grease. She said, "There's no such thing as an ordinary Sunday. Sunday is the special day the Lord hath made."

"How about the other six days of the week?" Callie asked. "Why aren't they special?" She had finished the slaw and was rolling out her mama's chilled biscuit dough while taking out her cross feelings on her mama. Her morning sickness had worsened, and she could barely stand being around all that food. She didn't want her mama to guess that she was going to have a baby, because it was tied to darker secrets: She had a lover, she had no use for her husband any more, she was going to take their child and leave Russell and her family and all that she knew. The whole thing was too large to think about. It was like trying to visualize heaven and hell and purgatory. She placed the pan of biscuits in the hot oven.

At the sound of the telephone's two short rings, Callie dashed into the hall. She barely beat Russell to it. "Hello," she said into the mouthpiece.

"Callie." The first time she heard Clifton's voice speak her name over the phone gave her a thrill. She waved Russell away with her free hand.

"Yes," she breathed carefully, watching Russell turn and head back to the front of the house.

Her mama called from the kitchen. "Sister, you didn't finish cutting out the biscuits. There's enough dough for another pan."

"I can't talk," she whispered, her mouth as close as possible to the phone. "I'm not at home; I'm at my folks' place. We're on the same party line."

"I can hardly hear you," Clifton said. "Can you speak up?"

"You have the wrong number," Callie said, louder.

"Are you trying to tell me you can't talk now?"

"That's right."

"What time can I call you tomorrow?"

"After eight in the morning," she whispered again.

He must have heard that. He said, "Okay. I love you."

The only times he had said that to her before they were making love. She liked the calm, casual way he'd just said it. She didn't want to hang up the phone. As soon as she did, she realized she hadn't told him about the wallet, and he needed to know it was safe. There wasn't any rush to tell him about the baby.

When she got back to the kitchen, her mama said, "Who was that?"

"Wrong number." Before the older woman could say what Callie knew she would, that for a wrong number it sure took time, she added, "The connection was so bad I could barely hear the person on the other end, so it took awhile for both of us to figure out he wanted another number."

"Oh, it was a man calling?"

"No, it was one of those women who grow moustaches," Callie said.

Her mama didn't recognize the sarcasm. "How would you know? You couldn't see who it was."

"Because this person had a voice low enough to be a man's, and women with low voices like that usually have hair growing over their mouths."

Her mama quickly put her hand over her own mouth

where some fuzz had begun to sprout. "Is my voice getting lower?" she wailed.

"No, Mama." Callie tried to atone for her meanness as she said, "Anyway, Daddy would love you no matter what. Even if you did have a moustache."

Her mama rinsed her hands and dried them thoroughly with a dish towel. "To tell you the truth, Sister, I don't care whether he does or not, anymore. Marriage like that—with loving carryings-on—is for young folks like you, and believe me, it doesn't last long. In a few years Russell won't look at you any different than he'd look at a piece of furniture he's used to seeing. He'll still expect you-know-what but he won't really give you the time of day. He'll lavish more affection on that bird dog of his than he will on you." Her face registered no emotion at all.

Callie put her arms around her mama. Flour dust from their aprons puffed up and made a little cloud between them. She didn't see any need to say that her own marriage of two years was already like her mama's of twenty-five. Instead, she said: "Are you telling me that you haven't been happy since you married, Mama?"

Her mama turned back to the stove and busied herself arranging the crisp chicken pieces on a platter. "I wouldn't put it that strong. I've had happiness in spots, so to speak. There's a heap of pleasure to be had from church work, from bringing up children, even from frying up chicken for all of you and the preacher on Sundays. That's enough happiness for one lifetime, I reckon." She stepped back to admire the row of platters and serving dishes she had filled with her bounty: pickled peaches, green beans glazed with salt pork drippings and cooked 'til limp, fried chicken and a mountain of mashed potatoes.

Callie was sprinkling paprika over the cole slaw, thinking how pretty it looked in her grandmother's cut-glass bowl, when her mama glanced curiously at her and said, "But if you can find happiness for yourself in other ways than what I've had, then who am I to tell you not to?"

Callie wanted to tell her mama, right then, exactly what was going on in her life. But she didn't. Learning of Callie's other ways would break her mama's heart.

And anyway, they had to get all those dishes on the table before the hot things cooled off.

As usual, her mama invited the preacher to ask the blessing, although Callie's daddy had pointed out before that he was head of the household and had provided the food, therefore he should be the one to get it blessed. Callie closed her eyes and blocked out the preacher's words so she could think some of her own silently. She prayed that whatever she was doing was going to come out all right. She told God she didn't want to hurt Russell or her mama or Clifton's wife and his children, but on the other hand, she didn't want to give up Clifton. She still had her head down and her eyes shut when her brother Pete nudged her arm. "Pass that platter, Sister," he said. Then he looked around the table and said, "She's still praying after the Amen."

Everybody around the big, circular table was staring at her when she opened her eyes. "I'm sorry," Callie said, her cheeks burning.

The preacher leaned across the table toward her and said in his smooth, pulpit voice, "Miss Callie, I admire you for praying your own silent prayer. And I hope Brother Ames over at the Baptist Church appreciates your good Methodist training." After the others had left the room, except for Callie who was clearing the table, he was still there. His wife had gone back to the porch to sit and fan herself some more.

He glanced around to be sure no one was paying them

any attention. Her mama was running water in the sink and couldn't hear. "Callie Tatum," he said, and she heard her name as though it were being called out by the Lord, "I believe you have a weighty problem on your mind. My work on this earth is to help people. You used to be one of my own flock, and I hope you still feel at home with me. Will you come to my study one day soon, so we can have a private talk about what's troubling you?"

She couldn't think of anything to say. He took that for shyness, and patted her shoulder. "I'll be listening for your call," he said. "Whatever you choose to tell me, however you wish to unburden yourself, won't be heard by anyone else but our heavenly Father who knows all." He squeezed her hand and left the dining room.

Russell had Lucy and Mr. Will in the car and was blowing the horn for Callie to come on. She ran back to the kitchen where her mama was putting plates in the sink to soak. "Sorry I can't stay and help you clean up. Russell is having a fit to get going."

Her mama nodded, pleased that Callie knew better than to rile Russell. Her daddy was playing dominoes on the porch with Pete.

"Bye, Daddy," she said, throwing him a kiss in passing.

"Be a good girl, Callie," he said, without raising his eyes from the game. He had said that to her since she was Lucy's age.

"I'm not a girl anymore, I'm a woman," she called back.

They were just about to drive off when Pete yelled out, "Daddy says you're a smart aleck and your husband ought to whip your butt."

Russell heard that, and asked her did she think he should, but she didn't give him a reply. She didn't say another word. Russell whistled, and Mr. Will, his head sunk to his chest, snored noisily. Lucy was wedged between her and Russell, quietly sucking her thumb. Callie felt so closed in she wanted to get out and ride on the running board with the wind whipping against her. Clifton would never fit in with her dumb loud brothers and her aloof daddy who had no desire whatsoever to express himself in talk. Even her mama, now that she'd got fat and had that fuzz over her mouth, would shame her. If she moved to Birmingham with Clifton, she would have to figure out a way to leave her whole past life behind, except, of course, for Lucy.

Mr. Will suddenly awoke with a jerk. "Honor thy father and thy mother," he pronounced solemnly.

"What the hell," Russell groaned. "Looks like we're in for another sermon today."

But the old man didn't say any more; he put his head against the seat and went back to sleep. Callie wished he hadn't said those words. Just when some devil inside her told her she could go clear off across the state and leave her husband, as well as her father and her mother, some angel of the Lord inside Mr. Will spoke up and reminded her that she couldn't.

Callie nearly jumped out of her skin when the phone rang at exactly five past eight the next morning. Russell had been gone for over an hour; Lucy and Mr. Will were situated where they wouldn't bother her; and she was waiting right there by the telephone for Clifton's call. But when the ring cut through the sound of her own breathing, she looked around to be sure no one else was within earshot. Mr. Will and Lucy didn't count even if they did hear. Now that Russell had become convinced his daddy was demented, he wouldn't believe anything he said.

Clifton began to apologize the second she answered.

"Callie, forgive me for that call yesterday. I knew I was taking a chance since it was Sunday, and your husband wouldn't be at the mill. I hoped he'd be out tending to things on the farm."

"That's all right. No harm was done. But we're not safe now. Somebody on the party line could pick up at any minute. If you hear a click, don't say a word. By the way, you left your wallet at the little house."

"I figured that's what happened to it. I had stopped at a filling station about halfway back to Birmingham when I missed it. I had just enough in nickels and dimes to pay for the gas. I hope it didn't cause you problems."

Callie's heart settled down. They were having an ordinary conversation, like two friends, or a husband and a wife. She was getting used to him, sort of. But picturing his face while he talked dazzled her like noonday sunshine. "No one else saw it. I found it myself," she lied. "Should I wrap it up and mail it to you?"

"I'd rather come get it. I can get away on Wednesday. Is it safe for us to meet at your little house again? Are you sure no one can see us there from the big house or the highway?"

Callie said, "I'm pretty sure no one can see us from anywhere. We'll be extra careful." But she didn't know how they could be any more careful than they had been. Clifton would be horrified if he knew that Arletta had some idea of what was going on.

Arletta was her friend, but Rafe belonged to Russell, or might as well have. Rafe's family had worked for the Tatums since slavery time. Her mama once said it was a curious thing about Negroes: they could be as loyal to you as your own blood kin as long as they worked for you, but the minute they left or decided to leave, they dropped that loyalty as easily as stepping out of a worn-out garment.

That wouldn't apply to Arletta. She would never tell any-one what she knew about Callie and Clifton. Except her own husband. She well might share her knowledge with Rafe.

"Miss Callie's up to something," Arletta would say in her slow creamy voice as they sat on their rickety cabin porch in the evening, glad to be free of the white folks who crowded their daytimes.

"You mean she up to something with a man? That what you mean, girl?" Rafe, dusky as twilight, laughing.

"That's what I mean all right." Arletta would draw it out. "What she did is, she took him down to the little house. Stayed over an hour. I saw him, through the trees, drive off in a green car. Then in she come, all messed up and crazy with love. Love dripping off her like sorghum syrup off a spoon. She don't care nothing about Mr. Russell no more."

And of course Rafe could supply the hard evidence. Snooping around the little house, he had found Clifton's wallet.

Callie hardly heard Clifton as she imagined that conver-sation between Arletta and Rafe.

"Callie, are you still there?" Clifton had been talking about his work. He'd sold a big policy and would buy her a present with some of the money he made. What would she like—Evening in Paris perfume, or silk stockings?

She said, "I wouldn't know how to accept a gift from you. I couldn't."

"Well then, I won't bring you anything—yet," he said. "But someday I'll pick out things for you, and watch your face as you open my presents."

"Russell says long distance costs a lot. Can you afford it?"

"Depends on how you look at it," he said. "I can give up a package of Luckies for this call. Tell me, how's little Lucy?"

"Lucy's fine. How are your children?" To her, they were no more than paper dolls, pictures in his wallet. She tried to imagine them in the flesh, real children, standing outside her front door with their daddy, tugging on his hands, waiting to meet her. Waiting to hate her.

He said the boy had left for church camp and would be gone for a week. He didn't say so, but she heard it in his voice: he would miss his son. "Clifton, do you think your children would like me?" she asked.

"I'd want them to know you, but they would live with their mother after the divorce."

Divorce. The word was out, crackling with the hiss of a whip over the telephone wires. "How does it work? Getting a divorce?" She made herself say the word. She had never known anyone who was divorced, although the librarian's husband had left town one day years ago, never to return. The librarian wasn't divorced, though; she just didn't have a husband any more.

Clifton said, "I would have to ask Mary to get it on grounds of mental cruelty. If she knew about you, she might want to use worse grounds."

"What's worse than mental cruelty? That sounds awful enough."

He hesitated. "Adultery."

The click came. "Is that you, Mama?" Callie said quickly.

"Mrs. Compton here," said a prim voice. "To whom am I speaking?"

"This is Callie Tatum, Mrs. Compton." She almost introduced Clifton. "I'll end my call in just a moment, so you may have the line."

Silence, except she could hear Clifton breathing up there in Birmingham. Mrs. Compton hardly ever picked up when she was using the phone. But then, Callie hardly ever used the phone. Mrs. Compton was clearly waiting to hear the other person speak, but Clifton wasn't going to oblige. After a couple of seconds, Mrs. Compton said, "Well, take your time. My call can wait." After they heard her hang up, Clifton said, very business-like, "See you Wednesday, then. What time?"

"Ten again, same place." Callie spoke fast, hoping she sounded business-like too.

"Is there anywhere else we could meet?"

"Not that I know of." She couldn't drive a car well enough to get places by herself. She would ask Russell to start back teaching her how to drive.

"Okay. See you at ten at our honeymoon house."

Callie winced hearing him call it that. Mrs. Compton had not picked up the phone again, but he shouldn't take such a chance.

While she prepared lunch with Mr. Will's watchful eyes following her around the kitchen, she kept hearing the word "adultery" in her mind as Clifton had spoken it. She knew what the Bible had to say about it: Thou shalt not commit it.

She spooned mashed sweet potatoes onto Mr. Will's plate and said, "You know a lot about the Bible. I wish you'd explain to me, in plain language, just what adultery is." She said it like she was asking him to tell her what time of day it was. She'd decided to risk opening up that hornet's nest subject of harlots and whores again.

He stared at her like he had trouble remembering who she was. Then he said, frowning with concentration, "Well, adultery is bad business. It's when a man gets dissatisfied with the wife he took to himself, to honor and cherish, and starts to mess around with some other man's wife. It's stealing, in the eyes of the world, and it rouses the wrath of Jehovah like no other sin. Not even murder angers Jehovah like the sin of adultery."

The next question popped out without being planned. "Have you ever known anyone who committed the sin of adultery?"

He shifted his gaze down to the sweet potatoes. His shoulders twitched. "It was a long time ago," he muttered. "When Miss Ruth found out about us, she went straight-away and told the preacher, and that so-and-so said I couldn't come back to church 'til I confessed. Not just to him in private. He said I had to stand up in front of the whole congregation on a Sunday and admit I'd sinned, so they could all pray together for my forgiveness. I wasn't about to make any kind of public confession. I figured my forgiveness was between me and the Lord anyway. So I never set foot in that church again 'til after that preacher died and we got the new one."

"Ah, Mr. Will," she said. "I'm sorry."

"You want to know what the word means? Adultery means misery. Lowest kind of misery you can get. It's like being in a swamp bed of quicksand; you don't see a way out. Once you do get out, and look back, you see yourself as having been crazy. And everybody else sees you as slime from then on." His voice had sunk to a whisper.

Neither he nor Callie had much appetite after that. As she was scraping food off the plates—Russell would take the scraps out to the dog pen that evening—Mr. Will began to cry. Callie knelt beside his chair and said, "Can you tell me what's wrong?"

"I should have run off with her like she wanted."

"Who was she?"

She had wiped his tears away but his eyes still glistened with wetness. "You ain't gonna tell anybody?"

"I promise I won't."

"Lizzie Compton." His mouth twisted into a shame-faced grin.

Callie was still kneeling by his chair. She almost fell over in surprise. The same Mrs. Compton who was on their party line; one of the ladies in the Methodist Church Missionary Society with her mama. She ran the general store a few miles up the road. "Mrs. Compton!" Callie said. "Why, she's a nice lady. I'll invite her to come by and have iced tea with us one afternoon. Would you like that?"

"Naw. Don't do it. No reason to try to stoke those old ashes again," he said. "She's back to just being Luke Compton's wife, or widow she is now, and it don't matter one whit to me no more nor to her, I'm sure, what we had together for a little while all those years ago. My wife would turn over in her grave if that woman, as she called her, ever came to this house. Miss Ruth never spoke Lizzie's name or spoke to Lizzie again after that terrible day she caught us, but because of her mule-headed pride my wife never told anyone but the preacher, I'm sure of that. I don't believe Luke ever learned of his wife's transgression with me. Even that preacher had enough sense not to tell him. Lizzie wasn't a member of his flock, and I don't know whether she got in trouble with her own church or not."

"What would her husband have done if he'd found out?" She whispered the question, but the words of it seemed weighted.

"Same as any man would've. He'd have blown my brains out with his shotgun, and probably hers, too. That's what was so crazy about the whole thing. It was dangerous as wildfire, and we both knew it. But once it started, I couldn't seem to make myself bring it to a halt."

"Then how did it stop?" She couldn't put an end to her questions, even though it embarrassed her to be hearing his confession, and she thought it probably wasn't good for him to be dredging up old guilt. It was the most sense he'd made in a long time so it was bound to be true, not something he'd dreamed up.

"Lizzie told me one afternoon, soon as I arrived, that it would be the last time. But it would have ended then anyway, because that was the day my wife caught us. She hitched up the wagon and drove herself up the road, hoping with all her heart, she later said, that she wouldn't find me locked in the back room of Compton's Store with Luke Compton's wife. Just as she feared, no one was behind the counter when she went in. She tiptoed to that door and put her ear to it, heard our sweet talk, the sounds we made—and when we came out, she looked at both of us with such downright contempt that I think I shrank a whole inch in those seconds. But as I said, Lizzie had already told me with all firmness that it would be the last time. It's the woman, usually, who comes to her senses first and calls things to a halt, 'cause she's the one with the most to lose. Unless, like I said, the man she's messing around with loses his life at the hands of her husband."

Callie could see them in the little box of a store like actors on a stage. "Did Miss Ruth pitch a fit right there on the spot?" She remembered her late mother-in-law as having a good bit of spunk. Miss Ruth wouldn't have taken it lying down when she found out her husband was carrying on with another woman.

"No, she was very dignified, I have to hand her that. She didn't say a word to me. She told Lizzie what she thought of her, though. She called her a harlot and a Jezebel, and Lizzie's face turned red as the inside of a watermelon, but she didn't flinch; she took it like she thought it was her due. It took me a long time to get back in my wife's good graces, if ever I did." He paused to take a deep breath. All this talk, the only confession he'd ever done, was wearing him out. "But what I miss is what might have been, if Lizzie and I had just taken what we had—that powerful feeling between us—

and gone away together, started up some place far from around here."

"You mean get a divorce? Both of you?"

His face stiffened with alarm. "Hell, no! Don't anybody get divorced! Never had one in the family!"

"But you couldn't have married Mrs. Compton without first divorcing Miss Ruth."

"I never said nothing about getting married again," he said crossly. "That would just compound the sin. Man takes himself a wife, it's 'til death do them part." He slumped down in his chair. Callie knew he'd finished talking. After she wheeled him into his bedroom and helped him onto the bed he took a nap that lasted most of the afternoon.

She got out a remnant of pink and white checked gingham she'd bought over a month before and cut out a sunsuit for Lucy. By sundown she had stitched it up and trimmed it with rickrack. Lucy played around on the floor, humming with the whirring of the foot pedal on the Singer machine. Callie put the finished sunsuit on her. "Now don't you look sweet as pie, all ready for Daddy," she said.

Sewing occupied her mind so there wasn't much space left for thinking about her predicament. By the time she heard Russell's truck grinding its way around to the back of the house, Clifton seemed as far away as the number of miles between them.

7

Russell braked the truck so hard the tires screeched, scattering gravel in all directions. He stomped up the back steps and slammed the door behind him. She sensed his rage wasn't for her by his silence. He wasn't going to tell her why he was mad until she asked. "What's wrong?"

"Had a fight with the supervisor, that son of a bitch." He flung himself into a chair and put his head in his hands.

"You mean you hit each other?"

"Nah, but I should have slugged it out with him. We just yelled back and forth. I guess you could call it a heated argument."

"What about?"

"Nothing you'd understand. Forget it."

"Does that mean you might lose your job?" If he stopped working at the mill, he would spend whole days on the farm all the time. Clifton could never come to see her again. Callie waited, not breathing, for Russell to reply.

"Hell, no. He didn't hire me, and he can't fire me. But I might just up and quit." He looked at her as though he could read her thoughts. He got out the bottle of whiskey he kept in the pantry, poured some in a jelly glass and drank it down in one gulp. He wasn't a heavy drinker, so Callie was surprised, but she didn't say anything. He waved the empty glass toward the bucket of blackberries, which gleamed like dark rubies, on the table. "Where'd those come from?"

"There's a thicket by the little house. Lucy and I picked them this morning before it got so hot."

"What makes you want to go down there?" He took a swallow straight from the bottle and belched. The combination of the whiskey smell and the rudeness of the belch set her afloat with a queasy feeling.

She said sharply, "I just told you. Because I knew the berries would be ripe about now, and I wanted some for pies." She had gone there to see if she and Clifton had left any other evidence of having been in the little house besides the wallet. The first thing she noticed was a clear rectangular spot in the dust on the floor, the shape of the pallet Clifton had brought with him and spread out for them to lie on. On her hands and knees, she had wiped the floor with the hem of her dress enough to erase the shape, while Lucy climbed on her back.

"You left my daddy here by himself while you went off that far?" Russell's eyes narrowed. He had capped the whiskey bottle and put it back in the pantry.

"I gave him the dinner bell and told him to ring it if he needed me."

Russell said, "Well, a blackberry cobbler would taste mighty good. When you gonna make it?"

"Tomorrow." She would make two pies and save one to give to Clifton when he came the following day.

The whiskey had relaxed Russell. After supper he was in such a good humor that when she asked him to give her a driving lesson he said, "Sure. Why not?" Right then, before it got too dark, they put Mr. Will and the baby in the back seat so Russell could sit in front by Callie. After a little trouble getting the car cranked up she took off with a lurch. "Godamighty, Callie!" Russell yelled. "You got this car jumping like a jack rabbit." But he was patient as she practiced gear-shifting and braking. "Easy with that clutch, now, babe," he said. "Let it up and down slowly, and don't keep your foot on it all the time."

She didn't get it down smooth, with a rhythm to it like Russell had when he drove, but after she steered the car up and down the private road and turned it around in the yard a few times, Russell said, "Shoot, sugar, you drive better than half the fools on the road. I guess I can trust you to take it out for a little ways, like over to your mama's."

The Ford sedan mostly just gathered dust under the lean-to shed attached to the barn. Russell liked to drive his daddy's pickup truck, which was newer. When Rafe and Willie went with him to and from work at the mill, they rode in the back of the truck unless it was raining; he said he'd just as soon not have them inside the cab with him every day. Now Russell had said she could drive the car! She felt like she had when the teacher told her she was smart enough to go to college.

The next day, after she'd made the pies and set them out to cool on the back porch—not deep dish cobblers, which might look countrified and messy to Clifton, but neat, shallow pies with crisscrossed strips of pastry across the top, and carefully crimped edges that stood up like little ruffles—she herded Mr. Will and Lucy into the Ford. Mr. Will protested mildly as she maneuvered him from the wheel chair. He muttered, "I don't want to go," and "Just leave me be." Callie ignored him as she concentrated on shifting into reverse, backing out. The mules in the back of the barn put up a fierce racket, kicking the sides of their stalls and braying hysterically.

She drove the two miles up the highway to Compton's

Store without encountering another vehicle. She braked close to the store entrance and missed hitting the side of the small wooden building by a few inches. To be able to drive was a power, all right.

Mr. Will groaned. "How come we stopping here?"

"Because I need to pick up a few things. I'll just be a minute." She left him in the car with the windows cranked all the way down and took Lucy inside with her.

Mrs. Compton was behind the counter, standing guard over the cash register. Her son, who was about Russell's age and said to be not quite right in the head, was sprinkling dark red sweeping compound from a paper sack onto the floor. Callie saw at a glance that she was the only customer. She and Mrs. Compton nodded at each other and murmured their hellos in simultaneous greeting.

The walls of the store were floor-to-ceiling racks and shelves, with only a couple of small windows to let the daylight in. As she got accustomed to the gloom, she saw the door that had to be to the room where Mrs. Compton took Mr. Will all those years ago.

Callie couldn't recall having been to Compton's Store since she married Russell. They got their staples at Hill's Grocery in town. She had brought a dollar of her sugar bowl money. She reached for a sack of coffee as she mentally made a list of what she could buy with it from the prices displayed on a large poster. After the coffee, there'd be enough for a couple of spools of thread, a medium sized pail of lard, and maybe a wedge of light orange hoop cheese cut from the big wax-covered round.

"Don't believe I've seen you since you left your mama's house," Mrs. Compton said. "I heard you had a baby. I remember when you got married, although I wasn't invited to the wedding."

Callie said, "That had to be a mistake. I'm sure Mama

meant to put you on the list. Please do come to see us sometime now. You would be more than welcome."

The Compton boy was push-brooming the sweet-smelling particles of sweeping compound and the dirt it attracted near the front of the store. "How's old Will Tatum doing? I heard he had a stroke a while back," Mrs. Compton said as she watched her son, ready to criticize if he didn't do his job right.

"As a matter of fact, he's not doing too well. He's lonely, and he sure would like some company. You may have heard he can't walk at all." Callie waited hopefully.

"That so? Is his voice box paralyzed, too?" Mrs. Compton took a fly swatter and slapped it across the counter like a buggy whip, then used it to flick the dead fly to the floor. "Move on thisaway with that broom," she said, sharply, to her son.

"No, he can carry on a pretty good conversation."

Mrs. Compton snapped open a large paper sack for the items Callie had placed on the counter. She said, "Some folks make up all kinds of things after they've had strokes. Does he talk crazy?"

"Oh, no. He just talks about ordinary things." There was no point in that poor woman knowing that Mr. Will had told her about the long ago loving in the back room of her store. "He's waiting for me in the car. Would you care to come out and speak to him?"

Mrs. Compton shook her head firmly. "No, can't say as I would. I don't have anything to say to him." She didn't seem to have anything else to say to Callie either, not even a "Now you come on back to see us, you hear?" She cut the wedge of cheese and weighed it on the scales and charged Callie to the penny for the exact amount; she didn't throw in any extra, and she didn't give Lucy the candy cane for free like the man at Hill's did. After her purchases were totaled, Callie got two cents change from the dollar.

She wished she had thought to keep back a nickel to buy Mr. Will a cold bottle of Coca-Cola from the ice box. As she was leaving, Callie regarded Mrs. Compton boldly. Outwardly, she wasn't any different from other women her age. Her hair had gone gray and sparse and her waist had gone thick. Her skin was etched with webbed lines as if she'd spent the last forty years picking beans and cotton under a relentless sun instead of working inside that dismal store.

Mrs. Compton turned her back and began rearranging cans of snuff on the shelf behind her. When Callie opened the door to harsh daylight, the Compton boy flinched and put one hand over his eyes.

Mr. Will was almost lying down on the car seat. "You can stop hiding now. She's not coming out," she told him. He pretended to be asleep.

Back home, she called her mama on the phone to tell her that she was now officially driving.

"I don't believe it," her mama snorted. "You were too scared to take a chance and drive outside our yard by yourself."

Callie didn't remind her that they hadn't wanted her to drive then; gasoline was too precious to waste. In fact, her mama had just learned to drive a couple of years before. "Well, I'm taking chances now," Callie said. "I've been up to Compton's Store to do some shopping."

"Compton's? That was a real kindness on your part," her mama said. "I'm sure Lizzie needs the business. Most everybody goes to market in town now."

"I feel sorry for her. Why didn't you invite her to my wedding?"

"We're on the p-h-o-n-e. Same line she's on, matter of fact."

"Well, I imagine she can spell 'phone'," Callie said.

"You're right, I expect she can," her mama said, un-ruffled. She lowered her voice, as if that would keep some other party on the line from hearing her. "I guess you're old enough to know. The reason Lizzie Compton wasn't invited to your wedding is because she had the poor judgment to get herself talked about with a certain man we both know, but who shall be nameless. Nameless, but not blameless."

"If I had to guess, I'd say it was either my daddy or my daddy-in-law you're talking about."

"Let me tell you this, Sister. If it had been your own daddy, you can be sure I'd not have stayed in his house another single minute after I found out! But the wife of the man who shall be nameless just held her head up and pretended she didn't know the gossip. However, I recall hearing that the wronged woman did bare her soul to the Baptist preacher."

"So the Baptist preacher is the one who got the gossip started?" Callie asked.

"No such thing. Lizzie Compton and that man she got herself involved with are the ones started the gossip by doing what they did." Her mama's voice colored with indignation.

"What about Mr. Compton? Didn't he hear the talk sooner or later?"

"Come to think of it, I don't know whether he did or not. If he didn't have sense enough to figure out himself what was going on right under his nose, I'm surprised some busybody didn't tell him. But then, he was such a mild little man; maybe he simply chose not to notice, as long as his supper got put on the table, the store got tended while he was farming, and his children got taken care of." Her mama paused before she added, "And Lizzie certainly did all those things without missing a beat. I always liked her well enough. I didn't hold a personal grudge against her, but in view of the fact that the man was—" She stopped in midair. "Well, never mind," she said, briskly. "It's all water over the dam now. Those things happen, and end, and sometimes cause a lot of destruction. But in this instance maybe it didn't go on long enough to harm anyone except the two who committed the sin together. Of course they damaged their souls. I doubt they ever could be convinced of Jesus's forgiveness."

Callie was shaping a rejoinder when her mama said airily, "Well, Sister, we've tied up the line long enough," and hung up. She wasn't much of a gossip or a telephone talker herself, despite her know-it-all air.

Callie spent the rest of the day in a frenzy of activity. She shelled butterbeans, put lemons through the squeezer for lemonade, weeded the zinnia and petunia beds, folded a stack of Lucy's stiff, sun-dried diapers. She cleared thoughts of Clifton from her mind like she would brush cobwebs from the corners of windows. Birmingham could have been a million miles away. She had a new resolve to end her carrying-on with Clifton, just as Mrs. Compton had meant to end hers with Mr. Will, before Miss Ruth stepped in and ended it for her.

She didn't even worry about whether or not she was really expecting. The sickness that came in short-lived waves could have been just nervousness. That night, when Russell pulled her to him, she reminded herself that it was not only his right, it was her privilege, because he was her husband and a good, honest, hard-working man. She kept her eyes open, watching his dark shape move in the dimness above her. She even tried to help, tried to make a rhythm between them like there was between her and Clifton.

She whispered his name: "Russell," she said, "I love
you," just as he was coming to the finish. He gave the
shuddering sigh he always did, with a little laugh at the end
of it. After a minute, he said so softly she wasn't sure she
heard it, "I hope so."

The second they came apart and her body was her own
again, she was filled with a sudden vision of Clifton, like
fireworks seen from a distance, an explosion without
sound.

All the thoughts she had kept at bay crowded in,
demanded her attention. She tried to will the shade to roll
down over the open window across from the bed as though
that would shut out Clifton's presence, which always seemed
to waft in with moonlight. The shade stayed up, but it
might as well have been closed. No soft nighttime breezes
filtered through the window screen; she felt as though she
might suffocate, and not just from the heat. She had a hard
time getting to sleep. Later he was in her dreams. She woke
up expecting to find him beside her in the bed. Of course,
Clifton wasn't there, and neither was Russell. The cranky
rooster was making a racket, and although it was still more
dark than light, Russell was already out doing chores
before he left for his mill shift.

Arletta had wrung the chicken's neck and scalded the
carcass in the big black iron pot to loosen the feathers.
Callie waited until she could see her seated in the shade,
with the headless, lifeless chicken across her lap. Lucy
was in her sandpile, Mr. Will stashed under his own tree
nearby. The smell of wet, singed feathers caused Russell's
hound, penned up a good distance away, to bark
crooningly, like he did at the full moon. When she got
around to it, Arletta would stroll down there and throw

him the chicken's head to play with.

Callie could feel Arletta's curiosity as she came down the back steps with the extra pie in a cloth-covered basket and said, "I'll be back in a few minutes."

"Wanna go," Lucy called out, but Callie said, "Not now, baby. Mama will be back soon." She intended to give Clifton the pie, and his wallet that was in the deep pocket of her skirt, and a short speech which she had rehearsed silently in front of the dresser mirror. She hoped he would be happy about the baby they'd started together. She would be able to tell right away if he wasn't. In that case, she would release him altogether. She had a husband. The baby wouldn't be born out of wedlock.

It was a few minutes past ten when she got past the hedgerow and could see that Clifton hadn't arrived. She went inside the little house, sat down on the couch, felt the noisy springs bunch up beneath her, and waited. He must have had car trouble, or changed his mind. Then she heard the squish of tires on the twigs in the dry dust, the car door open and shut, his light footsteps on the porch, and then he was there, framed in the open doorway, with sunshine splashing over him.

She caught her breath at the sight of him. "I was afraid something had happened to you," she said.

He came to her and kissed her very gently. "I've just about lost my mind, trying to figure out what can be done about us. Callie—" he hesitated, holding a deep breath, and then released it all at once— "I simply can't bring myself to ask Mary to give me a divorce." He looked away from her. His face was as stony as if it had been carved on a statue.

"I can understand that," Callie said. "I don't think I could ask Russell for a divorce, either. Russell would think I had lost my mind." It wasn't her memorized speech.

"So what are we going to do?" He turned his face to hers

then; he watched her mouth open to give him more words, then he pressed his own against it so hard her teeth ached from the impact.

"Maybe we could just run away. Not get divorced, or married to each other, or anything so complicated. Just go away together, far away." She said it in a rush, between their frantic kisses.

He was taking his coat off, untying his tie. She helped him unbutton his shirt. "You deserve better than that," he said. "I'll think of something. We're not ending this." They stared at each other in comprehension. It was settled: it wasn't ending. Slowly, as though they had all the time in the world, they took off their clothes, folding and laying them aside in small, neat bundles. Finally, they were both standing up naked with all that sunlight from the open door and the windows spilling on them like a blessing, just looking at each other, ready to fall on each other. A loud ringing started at the big house, not the dinner bell she had given Mr. Will, but the big farm bell which always meant come quick.

"Something's wrong," she said, gasping to get her breath, unbalanced by the sudden interruption of desire. "I have to get back right now." She threw her clothes on, not taking time with the buttons and snaps, and started out with her sandals unbuckled; she remembered his wallet was in her pocket and tossed it to him as she left.

"I'll wait here," Clifton said. "You have to let me know what's happened, somehow. Or should I just leave and call you later?"

"Stay," she said over her shoulder. No matter what was happening at the house, she would get back there to him.

It took an eternity for her to run back through the meadow. She couldn't make her feet go fast enough, even after she stopped to buckle the sandals. Arletta was waiting for her where the yard began, hopping up and down, wringing her hands and shouting, "I can't find Lucy. She was right there in the sandbox, I hardly took my eyes off her, then I went in the house for a minute to put the chicken on the stove and next thing I knew, she done disappeared."

Callie ran to look through the latticework to the space beneath the back porch. There was no way the child could have gotten under there; the only door had a padlock on it. "Lucy, Lucy! Come here, baby!" she called. She ran toward the dog pen. The big spotted hound lay on his side, switching off flies with his tail; he'd given up, apparently, on getting the chicken's head.

Arletta was running in circles, calling on heaven: "Jesus, Lord, find the baby, don't forsake us!"

Mr. Will grumbled, as Callie flew past him, "What's all the pandemonium about?"

She didn't take time to answer him. She ran frantically everywhere she knew to look. To the hen coop—Lucy might try to gather eggs, but would she go that far by herself? Callie and Arletta reached the front yard from opposite sides of the house and were starting down the road as though in a race. Oh, surely she hasn't got to the highway, Callie prayed aloud. Then she saw Clifton, loping through the meadow carrying Lucy in his arms.

"Here's your baby, Callie. She's okay," he said proudly. Lucy was delighted to be the center of attention. She was dripping wet; her sunsuit looked pasted to her.

"Where'd you find her?" Callie said. Arletta grabbed Lucy from his arms as if Clifton was a kidnapper.

"I heard her talking to herself when I went outside the house to wait for you. I followed the sound to the stream and there she was, sitting in rocks in the shallow water, splashing around. I figured she'd got away from the house

and that's what the bell-ringing was about." He glanced
with curiosity at Arletta, who had collapsed in a heap on
the grass with Lucy in her lap.

"Oh, sweet Jesus, she could have drowned! Child done
followed you down there, that's what she did. Went after
her mama and nearly about lost her life." Arletta had
switched her accusing stare from Clifton to Callie. She
later explained to Callie that she was just trying not to
blame herself.

After his brief moment of triumph, Clifton was the one
feeling the blame. He looked like he was down-in-the-
mouth sick.

"Take Lucy to the house and get her in some dry
clothes," Callie said to Arletta. "Please," she added.

When Arletta had left with the baby, Clifton said, "That
colored woman was right; your baby could have drowned.
Maybe the incident is a warning to us. Do you want me to
stay away from you?" He had got his shirt and pants on
before he came up the hill with Lucy, but he hadn't
fastened all the buttons on his shirt. He was barefoot.
Callie was in a disheveled state, too. Arletta must have
thought the worst.

But the worst as far as Callie was concerned was that he
would stay away from her. Nothing in the world could
matter to her more than Lucy, but Lucy wasn't harmed.
Callie looked at him, at the question on his face: it was
entirely up to her, always had been. She smiled. "Let's go
back now." She took his hand in hers and they started to
run together, crushing thin pink and white buttercups
under their feet as they cut across the meadow, zigzagging
in their eagerness, trying to find the quickest way to the
little house. Callie felt a boundless energy; she knew
Clifton had it, too. They spent it all in a frenzy of lovemaking,
not on the couch or a pallet, but standing, leaning against

the wall, then locked together on the bare floor. When she got home it was after one o'clock. She was still so full of the time they had spent together, the talking (although she had not, after all, told him about the baby they'd begun) as well as the other, that she didn't hear what Arletta said to her. Arletta followed her to the door of the bedroom and repeated it.

"I said Rafe told me about finding that man's wallet at the little house, but don't worry, he won't tell Mr. Russell."

Callie said, "How do you know he won't?"

"'Cause it would shame Mr. Russell so bad, 'specially if he found out Rafe knew about you and that man before he knew himself, that he'd take it out on Rafe from now on."

"No, he wouldn't." But yes, he would. Russell would react that way.

Arletta went on, "And when Mr. Russell does find out about this monkey business you been up to, he's gonna kill the man what's been messing with his wife. You better put a stop to it, sugar."

"I went down there today to tell him it's over." She couldn't divulge his identity, even to Arletta.

"Well then, did you?"

"No, because I couldn't. Not yet." She ignored Arletta's reproachful gaze.

At supper that evening Mr. Will said, "A stranger came by the house today."

"What did he want?" Russell addressed Callie as though she had said it.

"He wanted to know where he could pick some blackberries. I didn't think you'd want strangers gathering berries on our place, so I just sold him that extra pie I made," she said.

"You're right, I don't want just anybody to come in and pick on the place, even if the berries are wild. But I'm sorry you sold that pie. I could have eaten the whole thing."

Clifton had said, when she gave him the pie, "I'll have to think of some way to explain it. I might just say Mary, this pie was sent to you by a lovely young lady I spent the morning making love with."

Callie smiled because he expected her to, but she didn't think it was funny. She was thinking, Mary, why don't you find someone else to cook for so I can cook for your husband? Mary, why don't you disappear from the face of the earth? Clifton probably threw the pie out on the side of the highway somewhere as he drove back to Birmingham. Buzzards ate it, or crows. And Russell would have relished every mouthful. Even though he took her for granted most ways, Russell did compliment her from time to time on her cooking.

8

"I can't afford for you to be out joy-riding every day," Russell complained. "Gasoline don't grow on trees." He had driven up in the truck right behind Callie in the car.

She said, "We just went over to Mama's."

"This sashaying around, showing off how you can drive, better not become a habit." He took the car key from her hand and dropped it into his pants pocket. "You can ask my permission next time you want to go somewhere."

"What if we had an emergency, and you weren't here?" The car key had always hung on a nail in the kitchen.

"What if you had one before you suddenly took up driving?"

"We're lucky I didn't." Callie held the wheelchair steady while Russell lifted Mr. Will into it. She and Russell could argue, snap at each other like puppies, and still perform a task together; that's where their rhythm was. "Your daddy certainly enjoyed getting out for a little ride," Callie added. He'd been left in the car at her mama's while she and Lucy visited, because there wasn't a ramp and her brothers weren't there to carry him inside.

"Yeah, well, he's not paying for the gas now," Russell said, as he struck a wooden match on the thick sole of his shoe to light the cigarette he'd just rolled. He cupped his hands over the spurt of fire, took a deep drag and blew it out in circles of smoke.

"You don't mind spending money on tobacco and cigarette papers for yourself, but you begrudge the price of a little gasoline so your daddy and your baby daughter can get out and see the countryside." She was becoming expert at arguing.

"My daddy knows every tree and fence post in this neck of the woods by heart, and my baby will learn what the countryside looks like soon enough, since she'll probably be viewing it for the rest of her life, too. And if you don't have enough to do around the house to keep you busy, well, then, I can sure fix that situation. Since you got all this free time to ride around, seems to me you don't need Arletta. If I let her go, we'd save some money for sure." He sat on the glider on the back porch, the cigarette dangling from his mouth, bouncing Lucy on his knee. Lucy tried to catch the smoke rings.

"Let's not fight in front of the baby." Callie sat beside him. Her bare arm touched his. He smelled of the strong dye used in the cloth that was woven on the mill looms, a different smell from what he'd had a year before, when at the end of a workday he came in from the fields. Then, he had the same odor of the wash after it had hung for hours on the clothesline. Russell sweated clean, not sour like some men.

"Who's fighting?" he said. "I'm just pointing out a few obvious facts to you about the cost of living which you seem to have forgotten. By the way, I'm fixing to rent the little house out."

"Rent it out?" He could have said blow it up and she wouldn't have been more surprised. "Who in the world would want to rent it?"

"A man I met who's working on the WPA project. They're rebuilding the bridge near the entrance to the mill. It's a good solid house, and he's damned glad to get it.

As I recall, you sure hated to leave that place."

"When would he move in?" They were having an ordinary conversation while part of her life caved in.

"Next week. I told him it wasn't furnished, except for a couch and a table. I guess he has some stuff of his own."

"I suppose he's married." Could she bear the thought of another woman living there?

"Got a wife and a couple of kids."

"It's too small for four people," she said.

"They been sharing a trailer with another family, so it'll look big to them."

"Are they gypsies?"

"Hell, no. I wouldn't rent to gypsies, they'd steal us blind," Russell said. "This man was tenant-farming in the next county and lost the place when the crops didn't come through. He got hit worse than we did, 'cause he didn't own his land. He moved over here with the bridge construction crew. He seems decent enough, just down on his luck. And anyway, it's done."

"All right," Callie said, and suddenly, it was all right. What Clifton had called their honeymoon house wouldn't be available to them any more. He couldn't come back and see her; she wouldn't get caught. She laughed, she was so relieved.

"What's funny?" Russell couldn't bear being laughed at, and wanted to make sure he wasn't.

"Nothing. I was remembering how it was when we lived there right after we married. It was like I finally got the play house I always wanted when I was a little girl."

"I never got anything I wanted when I was little," Russell said. "Nothing a-tall. I know one Christmas, I was about six, I wished hard as I knew how for a bicycle, and kept talking about it. I really thought I would get one under that little cedar bush with red and silver balls on it that my mama set up in the front hall. But nope, I didn't. On Christmas morning there was a bunch of candy canes and a slingshot in my sock and that was all for me, but Lela got the doll she wanted. I asked how come I didn't get a bicycle, and Daddy said we didn't have money enough for foolishness like that, and besides, we didn't even have a road smooth enough to ride one on."

"Well, you knew you'd have this farm one day," Callie said. "You always knew that."

"If it was really my farm, not still my daddy's and then going to be half mine with the other half belonging to my sister, you know what I'd do with this place?"

"What?"

"I'd sell the hell out of it and head up north, I swear I would."

"North?" Where did "north" begin? She saw blue-white drifts of snow in her mind and felt the chill in her heart. "What about me and Lucy?"

"Where I go, you go. That's what the good book says."

"I thought you liked being on land that had been in your family for five generations." She couldn't imagine Russell anywhere else. Not even moved into town, living in a house on a street with sidewalks. It was hard enough to visualize him working inside a mill factory that belonged to other people.

"I hate getting up before sunrise, breaking my back all day, year after year, and not have anything more to show for it than barely enough to get by. And some years not even that. I wish I'd had the sense to make something else of myself. It's too late now."

"No, it isn't. You're not exactly an old man. What else would you like to be?"

"Anything besides a redneck farmer and a loom operator in a cloth mill." He turned toward her with all the hurts of his lifetime on his face.

She comforted Russell that night; she took him in her arms, and, as confidently as she would knead bread dough, she directed the course of their lovemaking. When it was finished, she could feel his surprise, although she couldn't see his face in the darkness. She was caught up in his misery and his longing, and it was good not to be so occupied with her own for a change. If he wanted to get away from the farm, even leave the state of Alabama, then she would do all she could to help him. Russell was almost asleep, but she had to know something. She shook his shoulder until he opened one eye. "Has that man who wants to rent the little house ever seen it?"

"I offered to bring him out here yesterday on my lunch time and let him look it over, but he said shoot, he'd take it sight unseen, he was that glad to find a place."

The angel was still working for her. If Russell had brought the man to the little house at that time, they would have found her with her lover.

Clifton had left without letting her know how or when he would get in touch with her again. Maybe he was getting a sign of his own that whatever it was between them had to stop. Maybe next time he came or called he'd tell her it really was over.

∿

The next day, as Callie got out of bed, the bottom dropped out of her. Bright red blood fell to the floor as though poured from a ladle. When Russell saw it his face turned white. "My God, Callie," he said. "Is that the way you get your time of month?"

"It's never been this much before. I must be having a miscarriage."

Russell fetched towels and handed them to her. He

took the oilcloth off the kitchen table and spread it out on the bed. "Lie back down, hon. Who should I call? The doctor, or your mama?"

"Both, I guess," Callie said. He hadn't been that solicitous when she went into labor with Lucy.

Her mama arrived in minutes. She got a ladder-back chair from the kitchen and placed it upside down on the bed, in order to keep Callie's legs raised in a straight, slanted position. "You should have done that first thing," she said to Russell.

"He didn't know to, and neither did I," Callie said quickly. Russell didn't take well to criticism.

Her mama clucked, "You never even mentioned a thing to me. I was wondering if it wasn't time for you to have another baby. Well, maybe it's not too late to save it."

But the doctor said it appeared to have been a pretty clean sweep and he wouldn't need to scrape her out. He said she didn't have to go to the hospital, as long as she stayed in bed a day or so and didn't overdo it. After he and Russell and her mama had left the room, tears came as copiously as the blood had. When the crying spell ended, Callie felt drained of everything: blood, baby-making, tears. She had really wanted to have Clifton's baby, especially now that she knew she couldn't have Clifton.

Russell had gone to work and she'd been dozing when the telephone rang. Her mama came into the bedroom and said, "Someone named Clifton wants you to call him at this number. He said it's about some insurance. I told him you were sick in bed but he insisted he had to talk to you."

"I can't call him now," Callie said. She thought she might not ever get up again, the bed felt so good and she felt so weak.

"Well, of course you can't," her mama said. "What kind of insurance was he talking about?"

"I don't know. Well, yes, I do. It was life insurance. He called last week and I told him I might consider buying some." She couldn't even think, and yet the words came.

"Why on earth did you encourage a salesman like that?"

"He doesn't know I don't have any money. I guess I let him think I did. Is that so bad?" Callie lay with her eyes closed, following the conversation as if in a dream she hadn't fully waked up from.

"Yes, it is. It's dishonest, and a waste of your time and his." Her mama might have said more except that Lucy began to wail in the next room just then and she left to go tend to her.

Less than an hour later the phone rang again.

"Don't answer it," Callie called out, but her mama picked up the phone and shouted a cheerful hello. Callie said the Lord's Prayer aloud, to keep from hearing her mama's end of the conversation with Clifton. But she heard about it anyway.

Her mama came in and announced, "Sister, it was that same man. He said he had to talk to you right away, that the rate would be increasing and you needed to sign up now. I told him that I was your mother and could speak for you, and that you definitely were not interested in anything he had to offer, so he might as well stop pestering you."

"Thanks, Mama," Callie said, meaning it. The medicine the doctor had left was making her believe that nothing in the world was wrong. All she wanted was sleep.

When next she opened her eyes, her mama sat in a chair close by the bed. She said, "Callie, I'm asking you to tell me the straight truth now. Who is this man Clifton?"

"An insurance salesman."

"How well do you know him?"

"Not well."

"Then why were you repeating his name just now while

you were asleep?" Her mama said that like she had just won a game of Hearts.

"I must have been having a dream about what he looked like. He has a nice voice on the telephone, doesn't he?" Callie tried to make a joke of it.

But her mama chose not to see anything funny about it. "Don't you dare sign up for any insurance without talking to your husband about it first, do you hear? If that man Clifton had any sense at all, he'd know that most farmers are too hard up nowadays to buy insurance, anyway. How did he ever come to pick on you in the first place?"

"I guess he thought this big old house with all this land around it must mean the folks who lived here had money."

"So he actually came by here and saw the place?"

"Well, he might have." Callie couldn't remember whether she'd told her mama he had called her on the phone or had come to the house. She was getting a headache. "I'm tired of talking about it. My head hurts."

The next time the phone rang, her mama was in the back yard with Mr. Will and Lucy. Callie got herself to the hall and picked up the receiver. Even before she heard his voice, the wire emitted such a fierce buzzing sound she sensed something was wrong. Clifton sounded as though he had aged a hundred years. "You're not going to believe what's happened."

She could believe it, whatever it was. She knew it was something big: He'd gotten his sign, too. "Tell me."

"Mary killed herself last night."

Callie pressed her back against the wall and slid down to the floor. His words echoed in her brain as though he had called them through cupped hands into a well. "How'd she do that?" She waited for him to say it was a car accident. He didn't mean to say she killed herself, he meant to say she was killed.

He spoke again in the new, old man's voice that wasn't familiar to her. "She closed herself up in the kitchen and turned on the gas stove. She left a note, saying she didn't want to live knowing that I had betrayed her."

"Oh, Clifton. How awful." She sounded distant to herself. The hand that held the phone seemed carved of wood.

"Callie, there's more. With the note was that letter you had written to me, signed 'C', that I thought I had destroyed. I can't believe I left it in my shirt pocket, but I must have. Anyway, she obviously found it. And she never said a word to me. She cooked supper last night as usual. We had a meat loaf, and baked potatoes and green beans—"

Callie could visualize the supper table scene at Clifton's house in Birmingham: Mary, in a pretty apron, serving her own special meat loaf—did she put strips of bacon on top, or canned tomato sauce, or both? Mary would have known, as Callie did not, that Clifton's favorite dish was meat loaf. Callie heard herself ask, "Did she wash all the dishes, leave everything cleaned up?" Except the mess of herself.

"Yes, she did. The kitchen was spotless. Mary is—was—a perfectionist about housekeeping." He was proud of her. He went on, his voice controlled, saddened, as though he were telling a sympathetic gathering of neighbors and friends: "I found her myself. Thank God, the children weren't there; they were staying overnight with their grandmother. I had gone out to bowl right after supper. When I came home, it was too late; there she was."

Callie couldn't visualize Mary with her head in the oven, but she could see the room. It would have yellow walls and shiny green linoleum, like a kitchen in *Better Homes and Gardens*. Callie's kitchen had walls and ceiling of whitewashed pine planking. The only color was supplied by the large wall calendar that a feed company sent Russell each year at Christmas time, in scenic views of faraway waterfalls and snow-capped mountains. He was waiting for her to comment. All she could manage was, "I don't know what to say." Except damn Mary anyway.

Clifton continued with the details. "I tore up your letter and her note before I called the police. They didn't need the note to see it was suicide. The doctor said he wasn't surprised. He'd been treating her for a long time for her mental spells. But if I hadn't stayed out later than usual—I didn't want to go home early enough to find her awake because I have been avoiding sleeping with her since I got started with you—anyway, if I'd gone home about nine, which is when she expected me, I would have found her in time to save her."

"So you think she really didn't mean to kill herself, she just intended to scare you?"

"All I know for certain is I didn't get there in time to save her. It's like I'm her murderer, isn't it?" He wanted her to tell him everything would be all right, that it wasn't his fault.

She couldn't give him that reassurance, but she could shoulder the guilt with him. She said, "We're being punished. I've just had a miscarriage."

Several seconds went by before he said, coolly, "I assume it was your husband's."

Callie's face stung as though he'd slapped her. "It was yours, if that matters. The doctor said when someone loses a baby early on, it's usually nature's way of correcting a mistake." She heard her mama coming in the back door. "I have to stop now," she said. "My mama will be here for at least two days, so we can't talk again for awhile. Clifton, I'm sorry about what you're going through." She waited a second before hanging up to give him a chance to say he was sorry about what she was going through, too, but he didn't. She got back to the bed before her mama came in with a tall glass of Ovaltine mixed in cold milk.

"Drink this. The iron in it will build your blood supply back up. Now, hon, don't carry on so over this loss," her mama said, seeing new tears streaming down Callie's face. "You'll have more babies."

"No, I won't," Callie said. "Not like that one. That one was special."

"More special than Lucy? How could any baby be more special than your firstborn?"

Her mama was right. No baby of Clifton's could be any more special than the one she already had, with Russell. She needed her mama to jerk her up straight now and then.

∽

On the day after it all happened, probably the day of Clifton's wife's funeral in Birmingham, the Methodist preacher came to see her. Callie figured her mama had called him to tell him of her "illness." His face was kind and stern at the same time, like she imagined God would look. She pulled the sheet over her face, ashamed to let him see her.

"I hear you lost a little baby," he said gently. "That's a real sorrow for a young woman to bear." He sat down on the edge of the bed. Her mama had left them alone together.

Callie lowered the sheet to her chin. "Brother Johnson," she whispered, "I need a lot of forgiveness."

"Would you like to tell me about it?"

"No, sir," she said. "Not right now. I'm just not up to it."

"All right. But the time will come, and soon is my guess, when you will feel an urge to confess so strong that you will obey that inner voice. Remember: Methodists believe in complete forgiveness. I'm not so sure the Baptists do. So when you are ready to confess your sins, in order to make your peace with God, then come to me. Let me help you." He stood, closed his eyes, and placing his hand on her forehead, he prayed for her. Callie hoped her forgiveness would start with that prayer, but she didn't feel it; his solemn words droned above her like a distant swarm of bees.

9

"My sister lost a baby once, she close to three months along, and what come out of her look like pieces of calf's liver. It must have been the Lord's doing, taking away your unborn baby so soon. He trying to tell you something, maybe."

Callie acted as though she didn't hear her, but Arletta kept on anyway. "He trying to tell you that He don't want you making a baby with a man who's not your husband."

"Maybe it was my husband's. Remember what you promised and don't ever tell any of it to anybody. You understand, Arletta?" She didn't say "please, Arletta." She was giving orders. Her mama would have approved.

"You can be sure I ain't gonna tell. But I may not be the only one knows about you and that man." Arletta was working over the scrub board, her plump dark arms gloved past the elbows in thick white soap suds. "You got some mending to do here," she said, handing Callie a wet, wadded-up shirt of Russell's. "Two buttons missing and a pocket torn."

"I can't fix it 'til it's dry," Callie retorted irritably. She dropped the shirt into the tub of rinse water. "What's Rafe had to say about me?"

"Rafe ain't had nothing at all to say about you," Arletta said, not convincingly.

"Yes, he has. He told you about finding the wallet. He

told you he thought some man had been at the little house. Then he told you he thought the man was there to see me. Didn't he?" She hadn't raised her voice, but Arletta bent lower and scrubbed harder and faster.

"Miss Callie, we don't want no trouble with y'all. You our white folks. I'm with you, but if it came down to side taking, Rafe would have to take Mr. Russell's. I told Rafe it wasn't none of his business whose wallet that was and he better forget all about it, and I swear I think he has forgotten. He ain't say nothing more about it to me since the day he found it."

"I've come to my senses now, I really have." She said it with more conviction than she felt.

Arletta, however, nodded with satisfaction. "I knew you would. You too sensible to be playing with fire once you see how hot it is."

Inspired by Arletta's confidence in her, Callie determined to talk some sense into herself, even if she couldn't forgive herself like God could. As her mama had pointed out, the loss of a baby that had been inside her for such a brief time wasn't cause for her to go to pieces.

She was full of her new resolve. She spent a lot of time cuddling Lucy, squeezing her close 'til the child protested and pushed her away. She tried to talk to Russell about what all seemed to be bothering him, and she wanted to tell him what was bothering her—except there really wasn't anything she could tell him that didn't come back to the issue of another man being in her life—but Russell pushed her away too. At night he lay as far from her in the bed as possible.

"You act like I have the mumps or something," she said. She didn't want to make love or be touched in that way, but she would like the reassurance of lying against his back, feeling the solid wall of him.

"I can't forget the sight of you losing all that blood. The doctor was right when he said you shouldn't have kids close together. We should have waited longer." He patted her shoulder but that was as close as he would get.

A week went by that was as long as a year, except that nothing outwardly changed. She wanted the last days of summer to be over with, so a new season could begin, with the trees turning somber before shedding their leaves like old tears. August hung over the place like a stiff bed sheet that had dried too long on the line. She would be glad when winter came and killed the colors that made everything so bright and excited-looking.

She took out her sampler to work on and saw the letter from Clifton in the sewing basket. She read it again before she took a match to it and burned it to ashes. A sudden sorrow for him came upon her. She visualized him in a black suit, looking down at his wife's grave. She would write him a proper letter of sympathy, as a friend.

She wrote that she wished for him the very best, and hoped that, despite his deep grief at this time, he would think of her, if he did at all, with kindness, as she would of him. Writing it made her start to see his face. He was looking straight at her, not down at his wife's grave. She felt something warm inside where the baby they had started had been, and then she was remembering, remembering, remembering, and wishing, wishing, wishing she could be with him like that again. She carried the wish around, aware of it, not trying to push it aside. And yet, whenever the phone rang, and he wasn't on the other end of the line, she felt miraculously saved, as though by strong prayer.

She put the letter in the mailbox with the pennies for the stamp. She watched from the house for the postman until she saw him make his stop and drive on. If Clifton read between the lines, he would know what she was thinking about while she was writing to him. If he did not respond, she would know that he had resolved his feelings for her.

A couple of days later, she took Lucy by the hand and started toward the little house. She intended to pick more blackberries if the birds hadn't cleaned the vines. A battered old car with a grimy mattress rope-tied to the top of it was parked close to the house. Russell's friend had arrived and was moving in! Russell hadn't mentioned him to her again; she didn't even know the man's name.

"Morning," she called as all four of them came out of the house. The man wore overalls with no shirt underneath, and the children, scrawny and potbellied with scabs all over their legs, didn't have on a stitch except little scraps of underpants. The woman's face was as lumpy as a potato; her stomach was out in front of her enough to make her swaybacked. She looked to be about six months along. She spat on the ground, then eased herself down onto the running board of the car, holding her swollen middle like it was a pumpkin. The children, a boy and a girl, crawled onto the running board on either side of her and stuck their thumbs in their mouths. "I'm Russell's wife," Callie said. "He didn't tell me you all were moving in today. Guess he forgot."

"Matter of fact," the man said, "I haven't seen Russell lately. We just decided we'd come on, since he was expecting us to move in about now."

They appeared more poverty-stricken than anybody she'd seen in awhile. Callie started to tell them if they needed anything to come up to the big house and ask for it, but she didn't, because they might. She said, "I'll tell Russell you're here when he comes in." She took Lucy around to the side where the blackberry thicket was.

"You got any candy?" The children had followed them.

The boy asked the question while the girl snickered and jumped up and down. "We want us some candy right now," he added boldly.

"Candy! Give us candy!" the little girl chanted.

"I don't have any," Callie said. "And it's not nice manners to ask for things." He was a mean-looking little fellow. She didn't want to stay there long enough to gather berries. She picked Lucy up and started back toward the big house. She turned when she was halfway there and saw the children following. "Don't you set foot in our yard. You stay right down there, you hear?" They turned and fled.

Russell hadn't been home five minutes before he knew her reaction to the new tenants. He said, "I didn't figure him to move in without telling me for sure when he was coming. I haven't seen him around the bridge project last couple of days—he could have got laid off. But I expect he's good for a month's rent, and I'll get that from him soon. I already told him I had to have it in advance."

"It's a little late for getting it in advance. Lots of poor people manage to stay clean, but those Kellys don't even try."

"If you'd been living in a trailer camp where the water supply's not too plentiful, you'd be nasty, too," Russell said. The next day Callie told her mama about the renters. "You'll have to keep your screen doors latched now," her mama said. "Else those little urchins will be driving you crazy, coming right in on you."

After she hung up the phone she looked out back and there they were, poking and laughing at Mr. Will in his chair under the tree. Callie ran out. She stood close to Mr. Will and said, "Don't you dare bother him. I told you not to come around us, so why are you here?"

"We just wanted to see what yore place was like," the boy said. He grinned, showing rotten little stumps of teeth.

He couldn't have been over eight. The girl was maybe five or six.

Lucy was in the sandbox. The girl went over and took her toy shovel and bucket away from her, and Lucy started to cry. Callie whirled around and snatched the things back from the girl. "Look here, both of you! Just because your folks are renting from us doesn't mean you can come around here and bother us. Go on back now. Scat." She waved her arms at them as if they were chickens.

The boy took a good-sized rock from his pocket and tossed it from one hand to the other. "If I was to throw this at the old man," he said cheerfully, "I could hit him from here and knock his ugly old eye clean outa his head."

As if that were her cue, the girl pushed Lucy over backwards. Callie swooped Lucy up with one arm, then slapped the boy's face hard enough to leave the print of her fingers on it. "Go on home," she said, immediately wishing she hadn't said the word "home." The girl was jumping around, acting crazy, but the boy was the one she really was afraid of. "Your daddy is going to hear about this," Callie added.

"Damn right he is, 'cause I'm gonna tell him, and he'll come up here and whup you." The boy spoke like an adult. As soon as he ran off, though, he started to yelp childishly: "Help, Daddy, help! This lady's done hit me side of my head!"

The girl scampered after him. Callie got Mr. Will and Lucy into the house and latched both screen doors. Minutes later, a heavy banging started at the back door. "Who's there?" she called from the kitchen.

"It's me, ma'am. Sam Kelly, your neighbor."

Not her neighbor, Russell's mistake. "What do you want?"

"I want to know why you hit my boy. Now you come on

out here and tell me about it." He didn't sound threatening. Callie faced him through the screen. "Your children were cruel to my father-in-law, who's crippled," she said. "Your boy picked up a rock and said he was going to hit him with it."

"Aw, you know how kids is, always teasing. He didn't mean nothing, he was just talking big. That warn't no cause for you to slap him 'cross his face like that." His eyes and long greasy hair were black as chimney soot. Layers of dirt, in shades of brown and gray, covered his bare skin and overalls. Callie found herself staring at him in fascinated revulsion.

"I'm not going to apologize to you," she said. "And I'm telling you now, I want you to keep your children away from this house. After my husband learns about this, I expect he'll ask you to move on."

His hand touched the knob of the screen door, but he must have seen it was latched from the inside. He didn't try to pull it open. "Now don't you do that, Miz Tatum." He spoke as though she'd really hurt his feelings. "I waited by his truck for Russell this morning, to give him the money for two weeks' rent. My wife loves that little house to pieces already. Why, she's done washed those old dirty curtains you had in there. She's cleaning the place up where it looks real nice."

Callie should have washed and ironed the curtains, not for the Kellys, but for Clifton. "I mean for you to keep your children away from this house."

The man smiled and said softly, "You really are a queen, Miz Tatum, with that fine dark hair. You're as pretty as that movie star, Loretta Young."

She turned and walked into the kitchen as though she hadn't heard him. She watched through the window until he left, then she locked both the solid outside doors and re-latched the inner screen doors. When Russell got home he said, "Why you got the place closed up like an oven? I told you, no matter how hot it is, you have to keep some cross ventilation. Only way to do that is to leave those outside doors open."

She told him what had happened. She saw from the expression on his face that he thought she was exaggerating, but she kept on. "I'm afraid of that man and his boy, Russell. Please get rid of them. I'm begging you." She was afraid of the little girl, too, but Russell really wouldn't believe that.

Russell picked up a bowl that held the remains of Lucy's soggy supper and threw it across the room against the wall. The pieces flew everywhere. She wouldn't stoop to clean it up while he was looking, although she'd have to do it sooner or later. He said, "You are stubborn crazy, is what you are. I am a pretty fair judge of character, and I happen to know that Sam Kelly has had some bad breaks, like lots of folks in our neck of the woods, and I wanted to do a Christian deed and help him out. But no, you got to go and act high and mighty. So his little girl just playful-like knocks our spoiled crybaby over in the sandpile. Then you insult his boy, and the boy lets you know he's no sissy, he can look out for himself. So the boy's daddy comes over to talk to you about it, and you insult him, too. I hope you're proud of yourself, Callie. You really take the cake, you do."

Her silence infuriated him more. He got his whiskey and grabbed one of the new jars of fig preserves. "I'm going down there and officially welcome the Kelly family. I'll tell them my missus sent them a gift of her own fancy cooking. Maybe that will undo some of the damage you did."

"Please don't, Russell. They're dangerous. Wait until tomorrow, and then tell them they have to leave."

"Shut up, Callie." He pointed the bottle at her as though it were a gun. "This subject is closed." He slammed the door on his way out. The truck roared off like a wounded animal as he jammed his foot hard on the gas. She watched the beams from his headlights slice the darkness with slivers of yellow light. He didn't come back until after midnight. He filled the house with the fact of his drunkenness. He fell onto the bed beside her, and she was the one that night who clung to the edge of the mattress, putting as much distance as possible between them.

❧

She dropped a basket of fresh-dried clothes in her haste to get to the phone. She knew it would be Clifton. "You okay, Callie? Are you over that sickness?"

"Yes. I'm fine now." But he was the sickness, and she wasn't over it.

"That's good. I got your letter. Thanks for writing. Would you like for me to come back and see you?" As though he were asking for permission to play out after dark.

"Haven't we caused something so bad that you wouldn't want to see me anymore?" She wanted him to say nothing was so bad that he wouldn't want to see her again, even the fact that his children's mother was dead because of her.

There was that childish petulant lilt to his voice again. "I want to see you." Like he was saying, "I want to take rat poison."

"Clifton, seeing me would be a reminder of what your wife did, because of us. I don't want to see blame in your eyes."

"Don't even think like that. I have a lot of things to tell you, and not over the telephone." As he said that she heard someone pick up on the line.

"Not now," she warned, and put her hand on the hook, breaking the connection. She hadn't had a chance to tell him about the Kelly family being in the little house, and it didn't occur to her that he would just go there without calling her again. But that's what he did.

Later, he reconstructed the scene for her. The day after that unfinished conversation, he drove over mountains and through valleys, thinking only of seeing her again. He always felt, he told her, like he was embarking on a long voyage when he started out to see her, and he was always surprised that it took just a little over an hour to get from his office building (six stories high) in downtown Birmingham to her father-in-law's farm on a lonely stretch of resurfaced highway between two small towns. When no one came to the door at the big house, he drove on over the trail to the little house. Sam Kelly was sawing up a dead tree in front of the place. (Russell had given him that chore to do since it turned out the man didn't have a job anymore.) Clifton took in the beat-up car, the raggedy clothes hanging on a makeshift line, and a strange man in overalls and no shirt out there sawing on that tree. He said, "What are you doing here?"

The man stopped sawing and spat a dark brown stream of tobacco juice that landed near the wingtip of one of Clifton's polished shoes. "What does it look like I'm doing, friend?"

Clifton said, "Have you moved into this house?"

Sam Kelly looked him up and down and said, "Why do you want to know, mister?" Hearing that part, Callie wondered what Sam Kelly must have thought of the dapper stranger he was looking at so closely.

Clifton said, "I'm in the real estate business and I know for a fact that quite recently the place was unoccupied. The Tatums still own it, don't they?"

Sam Kelly smirked. "In a manner of speaking, they do."

Clifton couldn't figure out what was going on. "What's your name?" he asked.

Sam Kelly said, "What's yours?"

Clifton informed him it wasn't any of his concern who he was, and drove back to the big house. Callie, with Mr. Will and Lucy, was just returning. She had sneaked the car key from Russell's dresser drawer the night after he took it from her. She was so surprised to see Clifton's car she pressed the clutch and brake pedals too fast and lurched to a sudden stop. She thought she'd gotten past that clumsiness in her driving, and hoped Clifton hadn't noticed. Mr. Will sat like a statue beside her. She decided she would be impolite and not introduce him to Clifton.

But Clifton went straight to the old man's side of the car and said, in what Callie took to be his business voice, "Sir, I'm with Alabama's oldest insurance agency, and I would like to explain my policies to the lady of the house here. First, however, I'll help you, if I may, into your wheelchair." He eased Mr. Will out of the car and into the chair and began to steer it toward the ramp. Mr. Will tucked his head like an old turtle looking for his shell. As soon as they were inside, Clifton said, "Mrs. Tatum, I'd like a word with you now. My papers are in the car."

Lucy began to whimper when Callie put her in the playpen. Clifton unwrapped a stick of chewing gum and gave it to her. Callie pushed Mr. Will up to the card table where he could reach his checkers and radio. "I'll be right out front now," she assured him.

She said, as she walked with Clifton toward his car, "If Russell hears about this—"

"Don't worry so. Your father-in-law doesn't seem aware of what's going on. He probably won't remember anyone was here."

"I can't count on that. Sometimes he makes up things that sound a lot like the truth." She didn't want to waste the time talking about Mr. Will. The yearning for Clifton that had been locked up, coiled inside her, unwound. She could hardly bear to be so close to him and not touch him. The lowest limb of the chinaberry tree was just above his head; the feathery leaves touched his hair like someone else's teasing fingers. "I can't believe you came back," she said.

"Callie," he said her name the way he had that first day, as though he were trying out the sound of it. "I've missed you so." She thought he was reaching for her, but he leaned past her into the car window and brought out a yellow paper tablet. "If the old man happens to look out here, we would appear to be conducting a little business." He took a pencil from his shirt pocket and pointed to the blank lines on the tablet as though he were explaining the terms of a policy. What he explained was his new situation. "Everything is different now. After I heard your voice yesterday, it came to me that I'm really free to marry you. There is nothing, on my end, in the way. You'll have to get a divorce. But then, you would have anyway, after I got mine. Remember? We had agreed on that." His eyes burned into hers as fiercely as Sam Kelly's had.

"Russell would kill me before he'd let me divorce him."

"Is he violent by nature? Does he hit you?"

She heard again the crash of the china dish thrown against the wall. "He yells at me every now and then, but he's never raised a hand to me."

"Does he drink too much? I've heard men who live in the country can really put it away."

"Only time I've ever seen him drunk was a few nights ago. He'd been down there drinking with a man he rented the little house to. Russell came home and passed out."

"I just met that man," Clifton said. "Your new tenant

and I tried to size each other up, but we didn't exchange names."

"His name is Sam Kelly," she said, as though it mattered.

"Well, I don't think he'll mention my visit to your husband," Clifton said. "He thinks I'm a real estate salesman who might try to sell the place out from under him." Then he gave her the details of that meeting.

Callie was humiliated, having to admit to Clifton that such a man lived on the property. She said, "I have to go. Lucy might swallow that chewing gum. She never has had any before." But Clifton took both her hands in his, and suddenly there was that solid bridge between them, delicate yet strong, like a daisy chain.

"Please," he said, his voice husky. "Sit in the car with me for a little while. The baby and the old man will be all right in there for five more minutes."

She got in the car with him and they were all over each other in one of those minutes. She hadn't completely lost her mind though, and neither had he, because before they had any buttons undone he asked "Are you expecting anyone to drive up?" He had his hand on the top button of her blouse, waiting for her to give him the go-ahead.

"My mama might."

He moved away from her. "I want you to make Russell mad with you. Really angry—not so that he'd hurt you, but enough to start him drinking again."

"Why?" she asked, dreading to hear.

"Because this will be the grounds for your divorce: your husband is a low-down drunk who beats you. He won't remember that he didn't beat you if he was drunk at the time you claim he did."

"That wouldn't be fair to Russell," Callie said. "What about that other thing you told me about—mental cruelty?"

"Unfortunately, I found out that's not an option in the state of Alabama. And you have to stop thinking about what's fair to Russell. What happened to Mary wasn't fair to her, either."

Except that Mary chose what happened to her. And Clifton wouldn't be the one who had to get a divorce. She said, "I can't make Russell do anything. If he wants to get drunk, he will, and I can't stop him, but I can't make him do it, either."

Clifton's last words to her that day were like ropes lashing her to him. "You can make him so miserable that he can only find comfort in the bottle. Do it, Callie. Soon."

∾

"Your wife's gonna take out some life insurance on you, son," Mr. Will told Russell that night at the supper table. "She must think you're gonna get yourself killed."

Callie wasn't surprised. She'd been expecting him to come out with something. Russell looked at her. "What the devil is he talking about now?"

"He's your father, you figure it out."

Russell sighed. "So what are you talking about, Daddy? See if you can explain it to me."

The old man's eyes glinted with malice or regained intelligence or insanity, or a mixture of all three. "Well, son, your wife has seen fit to use your money to buy a policy from a city slicker in a green automobile."

Russell frowned at her. "Did somebody come by here today in a green car, selling life insurance?"

Callie shrugged her shoulders and said, with a sarcasm that she had to work at, because it didn't come naturally to her, "Why, I really don't remember. We get so many visitors out here I can hardly keep up with what they want or what color their cars are." She began to clear the supper dishes, making such a clatter both men winced.

Mr. Will said, high-pitched like an old woman, "You're as good as dead, boy. She'll have you buried in the grave-yard 'fore you know what hit you."

10

Arletta came to work with her lower lip poked out and her large chocolate-colored eyes smoldering. She didn't wait for Callie to ask her what was the matter. "Who them people ya'll got living in the little house?"

Callie said, "Some folks Russell saw fit to rent it out to, don't ask me why. Did they say something to you?" Arletta didn't go near the little house on her way to work in the morning. She always cut across the back field, which, as the crow would fly, was the closest route from the colored settlement called the Quarters where she lived.

"Two strange kids be standing out there near the hen coop when I came by. I kept on walking, without speaking, 'cause they looked like they was itching to start some smart talk with me." She paused, waiting for Callie to egg her on.

"What happened?" Her thoughts had been occupied with divorcing Russell. She had temporarily forgotten her other problem, the Kelly family.

"That little gal, she leaned out and spit at me. It surprised me, and I jumped aside. The boy started laughing hard, and I said, 'Now you didn't have no cause to spit on me, honey.' I said it nice and easy. And the gal say, 'Yes, I did, 'cause you a dirty nigger.' And then the boy chimed in and say, 'You a dirty, stinkin', filthy nigger.' And I tell you the truth, Miss Callie, I called them some more names, I mean. I couldn't stop myself. I called them white trash and some I wouldn't even repeat to you. I didn't holler, I stayed quiet-like, but I heaped a bunch of name-calling right back on them."

"I don't blame you." She wouldn't blame Arletta if she had expended all her pent-up fury at the white race on those two bad children. Which, apparently, she had.

Arletta continued, "I kept on walking my path, and didn't look back. I heard them run off, but they weren't laughing then. I bet they was going to steal your eggs, too."

"I expect they were," Callie agreed. She made up her mind right then to have it out with Russell again about the Kellys. He hadn't been back to the little house since the week before when he took his whiskey down there and came home drunk, and neither he nor she had brought up the subject of the Kellys since. Russell hadn't gone back to drink with Sam Kelly, which pleased Callie, even though it meant she had let Clifton down by not provoking her husband to drunkenness. She had tried to get him irritated with her, but he didn't keep up any argument she started. He was treating her nicer than he had in a long while.

"Arletta had to take some sass off those Kelly children, so she called them white trash, and a couple of other things," she told Russell as soon as he walked in the house, before he'd had a chance even to wash the mill dust off his face. "I told her I didn't blame her. They had no cause to abuse her."

Russell shrugged. "Down and out, dirt-poor folks like them got to have somebody to look down on besides each other, so they pick on the closest colored folks they can find. Arletta's got sense enough to see that, and she shouldn't pay those kids any mind. They're like gnats. Slap at 'em and they'll go away."

"His daddy sure didn't like it when I popped that boy

for bothering Mr. Will." She shuddered, remembering the
way Sam Kelly looked at her through the screen. First he
was angry, then he openly leered at her. She'd kept the
screen doors latched and a sharp eye out since, but as far
as she knew, neither he nor his children had been back
around the house.

Russell said, "Arletta should have ignored them. She
didn't have to hurt their feelings. Those folks are really
sensitive about being called white trash."

"Well, don't you think she's sensitive about being called
nigger?"

"That ain't the first time Arletta has been called that.
She's used to it by now. She's supposed to keep to her place
and not provoke white people, even what you and your
mama choose to call trashy white people. White's white
and colored's colored, and there's a difference. You've
about ruined Arletta by acting so chummy with her."

Callie said, "I need her as a woman friend." When
Russell laughed, as though she'd said something really
funny, she added, "I don't see girls I went to school with
except just to run into in town or at church." Even if she
did, she would rather talk to Arletta.

"That nigger, your so-called woman friend, was a sight
different when she worked for my mama. My mama taught
her everything she knows about cooking and cleaning and
keeping her place in a white woman's kitchen. Arletta did
the shuffle-step around white folks pretty well back then.
She's just got bold 'cause you don't know how to keep the
upper hand with her and show her who's boss."

"You make me sick, Russell," Callie said. Watching his
face redden, she thought, I'm mad enough now that I can
do it. I can make him want to get drunk again. "Now you do
some listening for a change. Arletta was minding her own
business. Those brats started it, and they were about to

steal our eggs, maybe even make off with a pullet. I'm asking you to tell that man he and his children not only have to leave us alone, they are to leave our hired help alone. I mean it, Russell, or else."

"Or else what?" He folded his arms across his chest and stuck his face close to hers.

Or else I will take our child and leave this place. She couldn't think of anything to say in place of that, so she kept her mouth shut.

He thought she was backing down. "I'll just forget you got wound up like that this time," he said. "Now, you get my supper on the table right away 'cause I got somewhere I got to go after I eat."

"Back down to your friend's house? Why don't you just take him the deed to it, sign it over to him, since you like him so much." Callie didn't make a move to get his supper, although everything was cooked and in pans ready for warming on the stove.

"I am going to warn you one more time, Callie, to hold your tongue with me. I won't take it. No woman in my house gives lip to her husband. What your daddy stands for in his house from your mouthy mama is not necessarily what I will stand for from you." One of his hands was balled into a fist.

"You going to hit me? That how you propose to keep me quiet in your house?" She emphasized the "your." Russell would hate being reminded it wasn't his house.

His mouth fell open like it was on a hinge. He snapped it shut, then opened it again and said, "If I have to, so help me, I'll knock you clean across this room, Callie, in order to teach you some respect. I would sure hate to have to resort to that, so I will accept your apology."

She said, "Well, you're not about to get one. The way I see it, I don't have anything to apologize for." If he

knocked her across the room, she'd have grounds for
divorcing him. Would once be enough, or would she have
to endure being knocked around several times to make the
accusation stick? Russell's temper was such that she could
lose her front teeth if he did hit her. Would Clifton want
her then? She tried not to flinch while she waited for the
blow.

By that time, both his hands were fists, and he was
shaking he was so mad with her, but he didn't say another
word or make a move toward her. He got his last bottle of
bootleg whiskey from the pantry. He didn't go but once
every six months to get a supply, and it had been almost
that long since his last trip. She watched him head off on
foot in the direction of the little house, plodding along
slowly, like he was an old man.

She was almost sorry Russell had left before he ate the
supper she had made. Pork chops and lady peas were
things he especially liked. She gave supper to Mr. Will and
Lucy, and then she rocked Lucy to sleep. She wheeled Mr.
Will into his room and left him there. Russell was responsible for getting him to bed. After she washed the dishes,
she turned on the radio and listened to Buddy Clark sing
a song about moonlight. She wondered how different it
would be to kiss Clifton in the moonlight instead of in the
daylight. She took out her stationery and got the fountain
pen and the ink bottle from the bureau drawer where
Russell kept his papers.

*Dear C–I hope it's all right for me to write you again at your
office. You never told me who's taking care of your children now,
or who cooks and keeps house for you. I know it must be very hard
for you to keep the home life going and make a living too.*

After she got that far, she couldn't think of anything

else that she felt she could actually write in a letter. What if Clifton's boy and girl were as mean as the Kelly boy and girl? That couldn't be. She had seen pictures of them. They didn't look like little monsters. She picked up the pen. Clifton would want to know what was going on with her.

At this very moment R. has gone off to drink with that man again. I did like you said and got him mad, but he didn't hit me. Please be careful calling me before you come next time. Remember that people who share our line can pick up and hear what we're saying. Also, the operator might listen in if she's not busy. Take care of yourself.

Sincerely,

C.

She couldn't sign the letter "Love, C." because he was still bereaved. How long would it be before he could marry again? People would expect him to; a man left alone had to find someone to care for his house and his children. But how long was the waiting period? And how long would a divorce take? She read what she'd written, then tore the letter up and flushed the pieces of paper down the toilet. She heard Russell rattling the back door and went to unlatch it for him. He came in, slumped against the wall, and waited until she allowed her gaze to meet his.

Then he said softly, "Callie, how come you're trying to drive me away from you?" His face was puffy with sorrow, tears that wouldn't be shed, the way he looked for days right after his mother died.

"I'm not." The lie floated between them like a balloon that might burst at any second. She walked away from him and sat down, so her face wouldn't be level with his. He came and sat on the floor by her chair and put his head in her lap. She could see he was not in the least bit drunk, but she asked him anyway. "Did you go off and drink whiskey with that man?"

"I didn't go there. I sat under a tree near the stream, and I took a few swigs from the bottle, and I meant to drink a whole lot more. But then I told myself that whiskey never solved nobody's problems. My daddy used to be a rascal in some ways, but drink never got the better of him although he liked a slug from time to time, and he warned me not to let it get to me. My main problem right now is trying to figure out how come you don't care anything about me any more. 'Cause I care for you more than I ever thought I could anybody." He had not lifted his head from her lap. His words were muffled in the cloth of her skirt, but she heard them clearly.

"I care for you, Russell," she said. "I really do. And I don't know what's the matter between us." That felt like the truth to her even though it wasn't.

She cradled Russell in her arms while he got his fill of her that night, but it was like she was off somewhere else, watching two people she didn't know. Not like when she was with Clifton, sunlight always finding them and streaming over them, as though it had picked them out especially. At night, the attic fan in the wide hallway stirred the air, making a soothing noise like angel wings overhead, keeping the fierceness of the dying summer lion at bay. But the heat from the bright days stayed inside her. The colors of that summertime erupted in her dreams, shaking into different shapes like a kaleidoscope, always with Clifton's face in the center.

She tried to remember how it was, how it had been for her, living married to Russell day in and day out before she knew there was another way to feel, before she knew there was a Clifton in the world for her. If she could remember that calm time and get it going again, maybe she wouldn't have to get the divorce and leave. She tried to pray about it, moving her lips silently while the sounds of the sleeping house surrounded her. But she couldn't find the right words, because she'd given up on the idea of a God who would come in and fix everything for her.

The next morning Russell told her he would see to it that Sam Kelly moved out at the end of the time he'd paid for. "I'll ride down there when I leave for work and ask him. Hell, I won't ask him, I'll tell him."

Callie said, "What reason will you give him?"

"Can't you leave that to me? I'll probably tell him that I'm henpecked and my wife says he's got to go." He smiled to show he didn't mean it. He left the house whistling cheerfully, something he hadn't done in a while.

Callie hardly had time to think about that turn of events before the phone rang. Now she could tell by the sound of the ring when it was going to be Clifton. Her mama said that Callie took after her grandmother in her ability to "see around corners." But Callie could not see around a single corner of where her own life was headed.

"Meet me in the park in that town near where you live," he said.

"Today? I'd have to bring the baby and Mr. Will." She hadn't driven all the way into town. She hadn't even got a driver's license.

Clifton said, "Can't you ask your mother to come over and stay with them? I need to be with you."

He told her he'd call her back in a few minutes to see if she'd been able to work it out. She was amazed at how smoothly it went. Her mama readily agreed to come over and stay after Callie told her the doctor wanted her to come to his office that day for a routine checkup. She hadn't been to him since the miscarriage.

The park was nothing more than a small grassy place on

the outskirts of Clearwater with a few picnic tables and
some rickety sliding boards and swing sets. It wasn't one of
the fine parks with rock walls and gravel paths that the
CCC had been building in other parts of the state. Callie
left her car behind some bushes and rode with Clifton in
his to the Shady Rest Tourist Camp a block away. The
street was empty, as though other cars and trucks and
wagons were making way for them. He had already gone
there to get the key to one of the cabins behind the small
cafe.

The cabin was dark and close. The bed sheets were
clean but mildewed, and the gaudy bedspread, centered
with a candlewicked peacock that stood out in red and
purple tufts of thread, had Coke-colored stains. Clifton
locked the door, then pulled the cracked, brittle window
shades down. A small fan on the dresser whined like an
out-of-tune banjo when he turned it on. He had brought a
bottle of pale yellow wine, a store-bought kind with a
printed paper label, not something made in someone's
kitchen.

"I broke the law by bringing this into a dry county," he
said, taking two small glasses from a sack. "So you have to
have some. We'll pretend it's champagne, and we're cel-
ebrating our engagement." He held out a lady's ring, with
a diamond in it almost twice the size of the one in the ring
Russell had given her. But the first time she saw Russell's,
it was in a velvet box. Clifton removed Russell's rings from
her finger, the thin gold wedding band as well as the one
with the little diamond. The cold metal of the ring he had
brought slid over her finger and closed around it. "See, it
fits perfectly," he said, pleased.

"Was this your wife's engagement ring?"

"I can't afford a new one. Don't let the fact that it was
hers matter to you."

She looked at the ring. The diamond shone dully, like a teardrop. "I think it would matter to her." She took it off and replaced her own rings. "Anyway, I'm still married to Russell. I can't be engaged to you."

"Well, you're going to leave him—aren't you?" Clifton didn't raise his voice, but she heard the sharp edge in it.

She said, "Not right now. I couldn't divorce Russell without having you available to guide me every step of the way." Without you, she thought, I wouldn't even have to worry about it, because I wouldn't dream of trying to get free. "You need more time with your children before you worry about my problems. Who takes care of them while you're at work?"

"Their grandmothers. My mother one week, Mary's the next. It's worked out all right so far. I have them at night and on week-ends."

"Both grandmothers live in Birmingham?"

"Yes. Close enough that the kids can walk from our house to either of theirs."

"Then you and Mary must have known each other forever," Callie said, sadly. The hours she and Clifton had been together, the only time they'd had to know each other, wouldn't fill up a whole day.

"We started first grade together," he said, also sadly, because he knew what she was thinking.

"Do you miss her?"

He looked at her with clear untroubled eyes. He did not think of himself as his wife's "murderer" now; Clifton had absolved himself of guilt. That fact had registered with Callie before he said, "No, I don't miss her. The doctor gave Mary medicine to cheer her up, but nothing did any good for long. She used to say that Lydia E. Pinkham's Female Tonic, which she could buy without a prescription, helped her more than anything else." Callie had seen a bottle of Pinkham's Tonic in her mama's medicine cabinet. She couldn't imagine her mama ever doing what Clifton's wife did.

Clifton poured the wine in the glasses. "Here's to us. To you and me and our three children, and to any we may have together."

She drank the wine in quick gulps, because she was feeling herself get as cold toward Clifton as she had been with Russell. Maybe the wine would help to loosen her up so they could do what they came to do. But it didn't, so she had to pretend, just as she did with Russell. When they had finished, and were silently putting their clothes on, Callie's eyes blurred with tears. She thought it had something to do with the wine, but Clifton thought she was crying because of him. He wiped her eyes with a corner of the bed sheet. "We'll be together soon," he said soothingly. "I'm going to read up some more on this divorce matter and then talk to a lawyer who has an office in the building where I work. Soon I'll be able to tell you exactly what you're to do."

Callie smoothed the sheets and pulled the heavy, ugly bedspread back in place. "You don't have to remake the bed," he said.

"I just don't want whoever comes in here to know what we were using this room for in the middle of the day."

He hugged her. "Callie, you really are an innocent."

No, she thought, I'm anything but. I'm guilty as hell. Men were lucky and could swear out loud. Women could only think in such words.

Clifton took her back to where they'd left the car. He waited for her to drive away first. The engine sputtered before it caught. She had barely gone a mile on the highway when she heard something like a pistol shot. Clifton had already passed her, tapping his horn and waving out the window; he was out of sight. The car lunged over to the shoulder of the road and stopped. The blown-out tire flopped around the rim of the wheel. Mrs. Compton's son pulled up beside her in a pickup truck a few minutes later and told her she was lucky the car didn't turn over. Since there wasn't a spare tire, the best he could do was give her a ride to their store, where she borrowed the phone to call her mama to come get her. Mrs. Compton didn't have much to say to her while she waited. Callie bought a package of mints and chewed up most of them. She didn't want her mama to smell that wine on her breath.

On the way home her mama had a lot to say about a man who would let his wife ride around in a dangerous old jalopy.

"Russell can't afford to buy us a new car. He says he can't afford gasoline for this one. I married him for better or for worse, and whenever I get the worse, I just have to live with it. Don't I?"

"Yes, hon, you sure do," her mama said cheerfully. "And I'm glad to hear you defend your husband to me, because to be frank, I thought you were having some bad times with your marriage."

"What made you think that?"

"For one thing, the way you were talking on the phone one day recently, according to Edna who claims she doesn't listen in except, you know, in passing. Edna says you were talking to some man in Birmingham. For another thing, I know you didn't go to the doctor's office today when you went to town, because I called there for you. I wanted you to stop by the hardware store and get me some clothesline cord." Her mama's voice was just as cool as if she had been re-telling her Sunday School lesson. Callie didn't say a word in reply. "Well," her mama resumed after a short pause, "I suppose this man in Birmingham is that insurance salesman?"

"I've had a couple of calls from him. And I have explained to him each time that we can't afford any insurance, but it looks like he won't take no for an answer."

"I see," her mama said in a way that indicated she saw the matter quite differently from the way it had been explained. "And why did you tell me you were going to the doctor and not go?"

"I just wanted to get away by myself for a few hours, and that was the only excuse I could think of."

Her mama drove in silence for a minute. "All right," she said then. "We'll say no more about it. I'll drop a strong hint to Edna that I will report her to the telephone office manager if she doesn't stop listening in on private conversations."

"Did she tell you what was said in the conversation?"

"She said she just happened to take note of the fact that there was a long distance call to your number from Birmingham, and you answered, and the voice on the other end was a man's. She didn't volunteer any more details and I didn't press her for any." Her mama added, changing the subject, "I think one of your brothers has been nipping muscadine wine in this truck. I sure smell it, don't you?"

"No ma'am. I really don't smell a thing."

Her mama had left Mr. Will and Lucy, who was asleep at the time, at the farm. When they got to the house, Lucy had fallen over in her crib and bumped her head, and Mr. Will couldn't do anything about it, and they were both upset. Callie got a piece of ice and held it on the red raised place on Lucy's forehead. Her mama's expression told her clearly whose fault it was. She said sternly, "Sister, your place is in this home you've made here. You chose what you wanted to do with your life, and you must stick to it, no matter what."

Callie wouldn't have been surprised if her mama had

slapped her hands like she used to when she misbehaved as a child. She reached in her purse to get a half-stick of gum for Lucy—even though she knew her mama wouldn't approve of that, either—and her hand found the ring that had belonged to Clifton's wife. He must have slipped it inside her purse when she wasn't looking. "Oh, dear God," she said in dismay.

Her mama nodded in approval. "I certainly think you have a need to call on God. If you won't confide in me, you can always take it to the Lord in prayer." What Callie heard behind those words was what her mama really wanted to say: "But you could try me first; I might give you just the advice you need to get out of whatever bad business you've gotten yourself into."

Not in a million years would she. She could not bear to see that face, as familiar to her as her own, register shock, horror, and disappointment, all at one time, in every fold and furrow. The really comforting thing about God, since He didn't always come up with answers, was that He didn't have a face. She could tell God all about betraying Russell by loving Clifton and not have to see His disapproval.

11

Later, she wondered why Russell hadn't asked Rafe or Willie to help him get the car from where she'd left it. As she told him about the blow-out, the colored men who had ridden with him from work were walking briskly to the Quarters, but they were still within shouting distance.

"Damnation, Callie," Russell said. "If it's not one thing it's another." At least he didn't chastise her for taking the car out again.

When he came up the back steps an hour later, Sam Kelly was right behind him. Russell said, loudly as though she were hard of hearing, "Sam went along to drive the car back for me. You sure blew that tire to kingdom come; must have been going mighty fast." He slapped her smartly across the backside to show Sam Kelly he could treat her that way. "Now, fix us some lemonade after all that trouble you put us to."

He had said he'd give the man notice to vacate the property, but he was treating him like a guest of honor in their home. "I don't have any lemons," she said.

"Well, how about a little ice water? You got that, don't you?"

She chipped the ice while they watched, both of them standing in the kitchen with their arms crossed and feet wide apart. The scents of their bodies came at her separately. Russell's was familiar, Sam Kelly's alien. They were like two steamed-up dogs after a bird hunt. She was praying Russell would not ask the man to stay for supper. Russell got uncomfortable after a few minutes of Callie's haughty silence, and steered Sam Kelly out. After the man had gone, Russell held up his hand, warning her not to come at him with any reprisal. "I know I told you I'd ask him to move out, and I will, but not just yet. He paid me the rent in advance that I asked for, and I spent the last of it just now buying a used tire for you. If I made him leave now, I'd owe him a refund. Anyway, I can use him to do some more odd jobs. He was a damned sight better at sawing those logs than Rafe or Willie would have been, and they've done got uppity now that they're hired regular at the mill. They think they're as good as I am."

Callie said, "I'd a whole lot rather have Rafe and Willie around the place when you're not here than that white man. I've told you, Sam Kelly looks at me funny."

Russell shook his head in wonder. "That imagination of yours takes the cake. He don't look at you one way or the other." He laughed, then said in a serious tone, "I'll go along with you this much. I won't give him any work to do that brings him anywhere near you, and I'll tell him his kids are not to have the run of the place, he's to keep them down there at all times. Now, the subject of Sam Kelly is closed until I reopen it. Got that, sugar?" He was still in a good humor, but his eyes were sharp, like they were when he went to trade his cotton.

"Yes," she said, not meekly. She knew he meant business. Next time she got in a tirade he really might hit her.

She was gathering eggs the next morning when the woman came up to her, clutching an empty cardboard shoe box. "I was wondering could I buy some eggs from you," she said. Her mouth twisted in and out of a weak smile.

Callie was gratified to see one of the Kelly family was timid around her. She held out her basket with a dozen eggs in it. "Here. You can have these."

"How much?" The woman had a dirty handkerchief with a few small coins tied in a corner of it.

Callie waved her money away. "No charge. But you'd best not count on getting any more from me, because what we don't need ourselves are spoken for by the market in town."

"Well, I sure thank you, ma'am," the woman said. She squatted and took the eggs one by one from the basket, placing them almost reverently in the box. Humped over the ground as she was, she looked as though somebody had beaten her down.

"You don't have to call me ma'am. My name's Callie." She added, because she was mildly curious, "What's yours?"

"Evie, short for Evelyn." The woman smiled openly that time, showing teeth that were as rotten as her children's.

Callie picked up her basket. "Well, goodbye, Evie." She had a sinking feeling. She shouldn't have exchanged first names with someone she intended to avoid.

Maybe God was answering her, after all. The idea flashed into her mind, whole, like a gift from someone else's mind, and she didn't even have to think it through. The way she would cut the connection between Clifton and herself was simple. She would have the telephone taken out. When Edna said "Number please?" and she gave the telephone company's number that she found in the phone book, the operator sniffed, "You got a complaint about your service, Callie?"

"Not exactly," Callie evaded.

Before noon a man came and unscrewed the oblong black box from the wall.

"How come he's taking the phone out?" Mr. Will didn't show any curiosity until the man was finishing up, wrapping the loose dead cord around the bell-shaped receiver. "Didn't Russell pay the bill?"

"Yes, but that's one monthly charge we won't have to worry about any more. It seemed a waste when all that ringing is usually for other people on the party line." There wasn't that much ringing, but Mr. Will seemed satisfied with her reasoning, or else he'd already lost interest.

Later that day Lela came storming into the house, mad as a wet hen. "What in the world do you mean, having the telephone service discontinued?" She always talked loud, and louder when she was upset. "I tried to call you, and Edna came on the line saying she had been informed by her office that my daddy's farm no longer had telephone service. As of this very morning. I told her there must be some mistake, but she said no, you'd had it cut off, all right. She heard you herself. What if there was an emergency, and I needed to get hold of y'all?"

"You could call my folks. Mama could get here in a matter of minutes."

"Callie, maybe you don't know it, but my daddy was the first farmer around here to sign up for telephone service. Disconnecting your phone is like telling the world you're poor."

She hadn't thought of it that way. She was going to stand her ground with Lela, though. She said firmly, "Russell complains about what things cost all the time. And this was the only way I could think of to cut down on expenses."

Her mama came over to find out what was going on, too. She cocked her head, aimed a beady-eyed stare at

Callie, like a curious robin. "Is that man in Birmingham still badgering you? That why you had the phone taken out of the house—to get him to leave you alone about that insurance?" The question marks hung in the air like clothespins on a line.

Callie was scared to look at her. She busied herself setting the table for supper as she explained, "That thing woke Lucy up from her naps; it bothered Mr. Will, too." He was listening. His eyes darted from Callie to her mama, and earlier from Callie to Lela, who never once even spoke to him. Lela had left, still mad, before the other woman arrived.

"That's right," Mr. Will spoke up then. "I got sick and tired of it ringing all the time. I told her to call the man and tell him to come get the fool thing, or else I'd take my shotgun and blow it clean off the wall."

Callie hadn't counted on that kind of support. She wished he'd come to her defense while Lela was there. After her mama left, she leaned over and gave him a hug. All of a sudden his hand, the one he could move, grabbed at her breast. "Mr. Will!" She scrambled out of his reach.

"Aw, what harm would a little quick feel do?"

Callie said, "Don't play innocent. I won't tell Russell this time, if you promise never to do anything like that again."

"You let that other fella do it." He pouted as though she'd snatched a piece of candy from him.

"What other fellow? What on earth are you talking about?"

"You know danged well who I'm talking about. That insurance man." He grinned at her, and held the hand out, groping again. "Come on over close here a minute, gal, let me have one good squeeze and that's all I'll ask for. If you do, I promise I won't tell your husband any of what all I know about you and that man."

For a split second, she thought, why not, if it'll keep him quiet. But then the shame of it hit her so hard she flung the dishrag she'd been holding onto the floor. "I don't care what you tell Russell of your made-up stuff. Tell him anything you want to," she said. "He thinks you're just a crazy old fool, anyway." That was enough to shut him up for the rest of the afternoon. The vacant look came back across his face. He didn't talk at all that night, not even to Russell.

Russell wasn't the least bit upset over the phone being gone. He didn't even mind that she hadn't consulted him first. "That's using your head, Callie," he said. "Since my mama died, we really haven't got the use out of that thing. I know you like to gab with your mama on it, but she's close enough practically for you to shout at her. Anyway, she comes by often enough so you don't have to visit on the phone with her."

The fact that she had unattached herself from the long magic cable that snaked along high in the air on creosote poles filled Callie with a new kind of elation. Joy, in her experience, had surfaced most exquisitely in loving Lucy—holding sweet baby flesh close; and loving Clifton—merging her flesh with his. Now she discovered that joy could come from the partial lifting of a burden. Marriage to Russell wasn't ever the burden that trying to become unmarried to him had turned out to be.

∽

She hadn't tried to guess what might happen when Clifton found he couldn't call the house. Three days later, he arrived in his Nash with the white-sidewalled tires. He came up on the porch and rang the doorbell. His face was as haggard as his voice had sounded when he told her about his wife's death. No one else was around except

Lucy; Mr. Will was in the backyard.

"I wish you hadn't sent the ring back," he said. "I wanted you to have it even though you can't wear it yet."

She had mailed the ring, rolled up in a scrap of soft cloth, in an ordinary envelope with no return address, no letter inside. She was glad to know it had reached him safely, although it hadn't occurred to her that it wouldn't. "You shouldn't have come," she said through the latched screen door. "I can't see you anymore. Please leave." She might have been talking to the Fuller Brush man, who was pretty hard to get rid of.

"You don't mean that," Clifton said, slowly, as if he were explaining something to a child. "There's a new life waiting for you with me, where you're supposed to be. You do not belong in this empty place."

"Empty?" Or did he mean awful? Callie wondered if her family looked to Clifton like the Kellys did to her. She picked Lucy up off the floor. The baby had jam on her face and crusty scabs from mosquito bites on her legs. "Lucy and I are pathetic, aren't we? I guess we look like what we are, dirt farming poor folks."

"I don't mean to offend you," he said. "But when we're married I'll see to it that both of you are dressed better than you are now."

"I don't care about having better clothes," she said, but she did care, especially for Lucy. She wanted to dress Lucy like a doll, in pretty store-bought things. He had hit a nerve. "You don't really know me. Let me tell you about who I am. My husband's father owns five hundred acres of land around this house. And my daddy owns land beyond that. I like not having to look out and see somebody else's house just a few yards away. I don't want to see some other woman's laundry flapping around on her line. And I'll tell you something else," she said, panting, she was so worked up, "I bet you think we have to go outside to the bathroom. Well, we don't. We have indoor plumbing here just like people in Birmingham or anywhere else." She didn't mention the septic tank that gave problems during periods of heavy rain.

Clifton was smiling like he enjoyed seeing her riled up that way. "I can vouch for your plumbing. I've used the bathroom in the little house."

She said miserably, "I can't leave my husband."

He tried to pull the screen door open. "Unlock this door, Callie."

"I don't think that would be a good idea. I'm truly sorry about your wife's death. And if I tried to go through with a divorce and marry you, I would always think it was my fault she killed herself. I'd be haunted by someone I never even knew." Callie took a breath, surprised she could get it that clear without having rehearsed it. "But if you leave me alone, even though I won't ever forget you, sooner or later I'll forget about her." No, she never would, but that shouldn't be Clifton's burden.

"Are you saying you don't intend to leave your husband?"

"That's right, I don't. At least not any time soon." She shifted Lucy to her other arm as the child flirted in her baby way with Clifton, who wasn't paying her the least bit of attention.

"Did you have your phone taken out so I couldn't call you anymore?"

"Yes."

He looked as if she'd hit him. "So you don't want me to come to see you again." He searched her face, his own almost touching the dusty grey wire screen in the door.

A lump had risen in Callie's throat that she couldn't

have got any more words past. She could only nod her head in affirmation.

He turned and walked across the porch, down the steps, got in his car and drove off, fast, like Russell did when he was mad. She watched the car right itself where the bumpy road ended and begin a fast, smooth roll on the highway; she watched until it was out of sight.

That night she dreamed of him, what little time she slept, and when she awoke the next morning and remembered she had sent him away forever she could hardly drag herself out of bed. Before, all her yearning for Clifton had blocked out her shame and guilt and fear. Now it was the reverse: shame and guilt and fear edged out the yearning. The powerful joy she felt when she cut the communication between them—as cleanly as if she'd taken her sewing scissors to a piece of crisp cloth—no longer sustained her.

The next day, while Arletta was there, Callie put on her most subdued outfit, a navy blue voile skirt with a high-necked white blouse, and went to pay a call on the Methodist preacher at the parsonage behind the church. Mrs. Johnson came to the door, her dress creased in wrinkles across her thick middle like furrows in a field. "Why, if it isn't Callie Tatum," she said, raising her eyebrows, narrowing her eyes. "What a surprise."

"Brother Johnson asked me to come by and have a talk with him when I felt like it. I've been kind of despondent since I had a miscarriage a while back," Callie explained.

"Well, come on in, then," the woman said.

The preacher told his wife not to disturb them. When they were alone, he said, "Miss Callie, I already know what's bothering you." He sat down heavily beside her on a sofa in his study, which had its own outside door. She could have got there without bothering his wife, if she'd known.

"You do?" She hadn't said a word yet except hello to him.

"I believe I do." He smiled at her as if they shared a delightful joke. "Tell me if I'm right. Your husband is away working long hours at the mill, and when he gets home and before he leaves each day he has to do chores around the place there, in order to keep that big farm from being closed down completely, and he's always too tired later to pay you any attention. He's been neglecting his pretty young wife. Isn't that a fact, now?"

"Not exactly," Callie said.

The smile hadn't budged. "So you got lonely, and lo and behold, another man appeared to comfort you. Isn't that a fact, too, now?" Perspiration had popped up on his forehead, although he was in the direct line of the floor fan.

"I didn't find him," she said. "I didn't go out looking for him. He more or less found me, but I don't think he was looking for me either." She kept her face averted and her eyes down so she wouldn't have to see the preacher while she was telling him the terrible truth.

He expelled a triumphant breath. "Ah. You found each other then, and you lay down together and fornicated, thereby committing adultery, did you not?" His voice was as soft as thunder.

"Yes, sir." Callie felt her face turn red.

"How many times?"

"Enough," she said. It hadn't occurred to her to keep count.

"Is he a man of these parts? Someone known to your husband and to me?"

"Oh, no. Russell doesn't know him, and you wouldn't, either. He's not from anywhere near here. And he's not coming back. I have ended it." Finally a note of pride crept into her voice. She couldn't look at the preacher, so she stared across the room at a big framed picture of Jesus that hung on the wall, and tried to absorb something from the blank kindness in the sad paper eyes that met her own.

"You have truly ended it with that man?"

"Yes, sir. I truly have."

The preacher took her face in his hands and turned it toward his. "Well, now, you've taken the first step all by yourself. And I am here to help you take the rest of the steps out of sin and degradation. Look at me, child. Listen carefully to what I have to say." He spaced the words out slow and heavy, like blows from a hammer: "As God's representative, I hereby officially forgive you, Callie Tatum, for the sins of fornication and adultery that you have committed with a stranger."

Clifton was never a stranger. But she didn't say it. She heard chimes from a clock somewhere strike the hour, as though the time was important: at three o'clock, her sins were wiped away.

The preacher confirmed it. "There! You see? You're forgiven! Feel that load of guilt leaving your heart! Let the goodness of God's mercy fill you from head to toe. Now, this is very important. Do not think for one minute that you must confess to your husband. There's no point in causing Russell to feel pain and unhappiness, is there? This will be our secret, yours and mine."

Callie relaxed against the back of the sofa. "You really won't tell Russell, or anyone else?"

"Of course I won't." He took her hand and squeezed it. He leaned closer to her face. "Now, I want you to tell me about it." He licked his lips. "Was it better than with your husband?"

Callie stood up quickly, but he still had a firm grip on her hand. "You shouldn't ask me a question like that," she said. Then he was standing, too, and before she realized what was happening—or while she realized it, like a bad dream that couldn't be stopped—he had her backed up to the wall, with her head against the glass-covered picture of Jesus. His breath reeked of onions and peppermint and wine. His belly, firm as a pregnant woman's, was jammed against her.

"I could stoke those fires that burn within you, and nobody would ever know," he whispered.

"I'll scream if you don't stop." She tried to push him away, especially the hand that was fast getting to the wrong place. For a fat man, he was much stronger than he looked.

"She won't hear. She's way off in another part of the house. Come back to the couch. I locked both doors."

The thought of the man's wife knowing what humiliation she was going through kept her from screaming, but also gave Callie a sudden surge of strength. She shoved him away and got to the outside door. As she worked with the latch to get it open, he grabbed at her every way he could.

"With me, it wouldn't be a sin, because I'm a MAN OF GOD. Don't you see?" As she plunged through the doorway to the outside world, she saw his pale, strange thing peeking like a curious bird from the opening in his pants. She held her ruined skirt, the waistband ripped and the buttons gone, to keep it from falling as she ran.

When she had the car moving, she began to laugh. She was thinking that of all the men's things she had seen—her brothers' when they were little boys, Russell's, Clifton's, and Mr. Will's, which was more shriveled than the rest of him, if that was possible—the Methodist preacher had the most ridiculous-looking one of all. In fact, it was the only one that made her want to laugh, and laugh. She laughed as she drove through town and beyond, on the lonely highway. But when she got home, her face was streaked with tears.

Arletta took in the condition of her clothes and said in a shocked whisper, "What done happened to you now, Miss Callie?"

"You won't believe it," Callie said. "The Methodist preacher, the one who married me to Russell, who eats lots of free meals at my mama's house, a man who's old enough to be my daddy, tried to—" She was about to say a word she'd never uttered before in her life, but Arletta interrupted.

"Yeah, most of them be bad about that. Preacher men always be after it."

Callie laughed that time without shedding a tear. Arletta joined in, giggling behind her hand, slapping her thigh with the other hand. "At my church," she went on, cutting her eyes around at Callie, "one sure fire way to be chosen to sing a solo is to go to bed with the preacher."

"You're kidding."

"It's the truth."

Arletta had a singing voice as smooth as fudge icing on a warm cake. "Do you want to sing a solo in church?" Callie knew better than to ask her if she already had.

"I would like to sing just once, out loud and clear and right by myself, not even with those others humming in the background, all the verses to 'Shall We Gather at the River.' But Rafe would kill me if he ever see me step to the front in the choir loft and raise my voice alone. 'Cause he'd know how I got permission to do it."

12

Summer was trying to come to an end. Occasionally a dancing breeze would cut into the midday heat clean as a knife. Once the crazy summer was done with, Callie reasoned, her spell of being so crazy in love would be done with, too. Clifton had not written or come back to see her. He had left her dreams; in fact, she didn't dream. Sleep fell on her like a heavy blanket that was hard to emerge from. She went about her chores, dragging them out, doing everything with a deliberate thoroughness, as though somebody was going to inspect her work and pass judgment on it. But she was the inspector. She had to please herself, make herself think she was good for something again. Better than good, even. She put up the last of the corn and okra from the garden, filling dozens of pint-sized Ball jars, and made egg custard pies flavored with nutmeg and brown sugar. She picked the late blooming zinnias, stripped the brown leaves from the stalks, leaving the perfection of bright, papery blossoms as symmetrical as windmills.

When Russell came in at dusk, she drank in the sight of him: he was her husband, and she would love him again, better than before. When he chose to make love to her, quickly and silently as always, she welcomed his closeness and made a prayer of it. She looked at Lucy with new eyes, too; she was a fairy tale child, pink and golden, on her way to being prettier than Shirley Temple. Even the constant presence of Mr. Will, who looked at her with an expression that changed from sorrowful to suspicious to uncomprehending to downright sweet, gave her a certain steady feeling of satisfaction. She drew strength and comfort from knowing she was the center of life inside the Tatum house.

And then the terrible events happened, on a morning that began like any other, with Mr. Will in his usual spot out back near where Callie was cutting flowers, with Lucy toddling around behind her. She turned to see Sam Kelly, standing a few feet away. He smelled like a week's worth of whiskey.

"Morning, Miz Tatum," he said. He slouched against a tree; his arms rested easily by his sides. "How you doin'?"

"What do you want?" In the flash of an instant his eyes had already told her things she didn't want to know.

"I come to tell you that me and my family are fixing to move on. My wife is packing up and we'll be leaving your place today." The boy and girl were behind him. Callie thought later that they must have known what their daddy had in mind. They looked scared and mean at the same time, but very solemn. No giggling or horsing around. Like he'd told them beforehand exactly how he wanted them to behave.

"Glad to hear it," Callie said. "I need the use of the little house again."

"I'll bet you do." He winked at her. "That's where you took your boy friend, ain't it?"

She had to act like she didn't hear him say that. She started past him; she had Lucy by the hand. She had almost got beyond him when he stepped out and blocked her way.

"I need a refund of some of that rent money I paid in advance," he said.

"Well, I can't give it to you. You paid my husband. I don't have any money."

"Come on now. I'm sure you got a sugar bowl full of silver dimes and quarters in the house. All you uppity farm ladies do. Not that you're any lady, though." He reached out and took the cutting shears from her flower basket and threw them on the ground near his children. The girl pounced on the shears as though she had a prize. The boy kept still, watching them.

"I'm going inside now," Callie said, taking care to keep her voice even. "Stand out of my way, please." Every time she tried to get past him, he shifted his position so she couldn't.

"Not 'til I get some of my money back," he said.

"You wait here. I'll take the baby in the house and get the money and bring it out to you." They were inches apart; when she backed up a step, he came forward. Even in her panic she had the feeling that they were doing planned steps together, in a practiced rhythm, like dancers in a picture show.

"Tell you what," he said lazily. He turned his head to the side and spat out a brown wad of tobacco. "My kids will keep an eye on your young'un while we both go inside."

"No," Callie said. She kept hold of Lucy's hand, but she had dropped the basket of flowers on the ground and had her other hand over her eyes so she wouldn't see him.

"Yeah," he said. He grabbed her wrist, started to pull her toward the steps. Mr. Will watched, his face all twisted and his eyes bugged out. Callie saw him rise from his chair in a sudden movement before he pitched forward. He fell face down on the ground.

"Please," she said, "I have to see about him—"

Sam Kelly slapped her, not too hard, as though he were giving her just a sample of what was to come. Lucy cried

out as though he had hit her. The boy moved quickly and
snatched Lucy from Callie and carried her screaming to
where his sister was.

"Leave my baby alone!" Callie finally got out the scream
that had been inside her throat.

"They ain't gonna hurt her, and I ain't gonna hurt you.
But you shut up that yelling, and come on inside now and
do as I say." She had heard that sometimes when people
really feared for their lives they got a super-human strength
from heaven to help them, but she didn't get any. She was
caved in with fright. She heard her pitiful screams like they
were someone else's. The hens began to squawk, the
hound in the pen howled, Lucy wailed at the top of her
lungs. Even blue jays in the pecan tree protested, with shrill
calls and wing-beating, swooping down toward them and
back again to the safety of high branches. He got her
inside, jerking and slapping her. Buttons bounced off her
dress like popcorn as he ripped it open. "You don't have to
give me any money. All I want for payment is what you
been handing out free and willing," he said, and when she
struggled he slapped her again so hard she almost passed
out. He kept talking, almost calmly, while he tore at her
clothes. "What you give that fella from Birmingham, and
the telephone man, and even tried to tempt the preacher
with, so I heard. Since the preacher didn't want it, I'll take
his share. You do it nice and sweet for me like you do those
others, I won't bruise you up. How about it, Miz Tatum?"

She hit him as hard as she could; she clawed his face
with her nails. When she scratched him hard enough to
draw blood, he drew back his fist and came at her face with
it like she was a man. She didn't believe it even when she
saw it coming. After the force of that blow she blacked out
enough to make the rest hazy.

When she came to, she was lying on the bare plank

floor. Lucy squatted beside her, patting her face, whimper-ing. Callie could see the baby was all right. They hadn't hurt her, and she hadn't been left outside where she could wander off. Callie raised her head and looked out through the screen. Mr. Will was lying in a still heap on the ground where he'd fallen. The man and his children weren't anywhere around. She got up, put Lucy in her crib and gave her some crackers. Her mind wasn't working on anything but the details of going through the motions of what she had to do. She opened the door and went out to see about Mr. Will. She had to make herself put one foot in front of the other, and creep, because she wanted to stay inside with the doors locked. The old man was breathing, but his eyes stared up at her like he didn't know her. She couldn't muster enough strength to get him up and into his wheel chair. Terrified, she moved into the yard 'til she could get a glimpse of the little house, with the Kellys' car still parked in front. They had not yet left! The sudden remembrance that she'd disconnected the telephone hit her almost as hard as the man's fist had. She cried then with rage and helplessness, and suddenly the numbness ended. She tasted blood from her split lips; her whole body ached. She took the big farm bell to the front porch and swung it back and forth, but she was too weak to get much of a sound from it. "Please, Mama," she cried. She couldn't stay outside. He might come back. She went in and locked the doors. She wanted to wash away some of the filth of what she'd been through, but she had to stay where she could see either door. She got the hammer and the big kitchen knife and crouched in the hall.

She heard a truck approach. She was as still as she could be, her life suspended in her throat. Russell came up the back steps, whistling. When she realized it was Russell, the stiff block of fear that had all but paralyzed her dissolved.

Her husband had come home. Everything would be all right. He must have turned and seen his daddy out there on the ground, because he exclaimed something and ran back down the steps. She got up to unlatch the door for him. Russell had the old man slung over his shoulder. "Oh, God," he said, when he saw her. He put his daddy on the glider and touched her shoulder. "What's happened to you?"

She told him, as briefly and calmly as she could.

"He did what?" Russell said, his voice thin. She repeated the whole sorry mess to him in even fewer words.

He ran his hands through his hair, frowning. "Why would he do that?"

"I don't know why." Her mind had become numb again. She still had the knife in one hand and the hammer in the other.

Russell looked from one to the other of her weapons; suddenly he whirled and staggered dizzily toward the kitchen. "Where's my gun? It's not on the rack."

"Then Sam Kelly must have taken it."

Russell's face looked as though it might come apart as he took in her bruises that were deepening to the color of eggplant. He said, "Don't you worry, Callie. I'll kill him with my bare hands."

"No," she said. "Let it go. Let them go. Once they're gone, everything will be all right."

"Nothing will ever be all right again," Russell said. He picked up the knife from the table where she'd laid it. "I could kill him with this," he said, matter-of-factly. "It'll just take longer."

"No," Callie repeated, but he moved past her and out the door. She watched as he went into the shed, as though he were about his usual end-of-day chores. He came out of it with the same axe that he had let Sam Kelly use to chop up the dead tree. Russell went past the dog pen, ignoring his hound's piteous howls of greeting. He had the axe in one hand and the knife in the other; he walked fast but heavily, with no spring at all in his step. She knew that he was afraid. Her own fear had gone over into him; she had let him take the whole burden of it from her. At the time, it seemed perfectly natural that he should go to confront the man who had wronged them, and that she should watch him go.

The crashing noise that minutes later blew dry leaves off the trees was as surprising as thunder on a day full of sunshine. She did not remember that the other man had the powerful weapon, the shotgun that stayed loaded and that, she had often heard Russell say with pride, would kill an elephant, if ever he needed to kill one. With his wood-chopping axe and a knife that had never severed anything bigger than a turkey's neck, Russell had walked down that path, past the Kellys' old rusty car, onto the narrow, foot-high strip of porch.

His voice had cut through birdsong and the machine-like whirring of locusts: "Sam Kelly, I'm here to kill you for what you did to my wife!"

Callie didn't actually see or hear him in that final moment. She was still rooted to the spot up the hill. Telling of it later, the eye witness Evie Kelly said that's what Russell called out as he stepped onto the porch of the little house. She also said that her husband didn't know what Russell was so all-fired mad about, because all Sam did to Miz Tatum was what she wanted, what plenty of other men had been doing to her.

But what Callie would hear in her mind were not those last words Russell ever spoke into the wind of this world, nor those words the Kelly woman put in everybody's mouths about her. What she would hear, maybe for the rest of her life, was the sound of the gun, blowing away part of her husband's head.

Callie's folks hadn't heard the big bell. What got them piled in the truck and over there in record time was the shotgun blast. Her brother said it sounded like the cannon in the Armistice Day Celebration. Nobody ever wasted ammunition shooting guns just for the fun of it, and hunting season hadn't begun. Callie was crouched in the front hall when they charged up the front steps.

Her daddy said, "Good God, what happened to you, Sister? Where's Russell?"

"Russell would be at work this time of day," her mama said sharply, as though he'd asked a foolish question. Callie hadn't yet wondered why Russell had come back home that morning. Arletta told her later that Rafe said Russell had forgotten some work gloves the supervisor had given him the day before; he'd started to go back for them right after he got to the mill, then decided to take off around lunch time so he wouldn't get his pay docked. Callie never even saw the gloves. Sam Kelly must have stolen them, too.

Her parents were waiting for her to explain. "Russell isn't at work," she told them. "He came home a while ago. He's gone to the little house to have a word with that man." She had not had to face the certainty of what had happened down there. She felt a dreadful peace in not knowing.

Her daddy's voice had a rise to it. "Did he take his gun?"

"The man had stolen his gun. That's part of what it was about, why he went to have a word with him," she said.

"Did your husband give you those bruises, or was it that man?" Her mama spoke very softly as she cleaned Callie's face with a damp washcloth. Her strokes were light and gentle.

"Russell has never hit me," Callie said, and felt a rush of

pride that she could make that statement. Her brothers stood near the doorway; they stared at her and blushed and looked away, then stared at her again.

"That man did this to you," her daddy's voice was flat. "Is that it, Sister?"

She nodded. Her mama took her in her arms and rocked her back and forth and started to hum the melody to a lullaby. "Hush little baby, don't say a word, Mama's going to buy you a mockingbird—" Callie could hear the words even though no one sang them. It seemed perfectly natural for her mama to be holding her as though she were a child.

Her daddy had brought his rifle. He and her brothers left the house without having to say where they were going. Outside, they began to trot, three abreast, her daddy in the middle with the rifle, toward the little house. They found Russell lying across the doorway. The Kellys would have had to step over his body when they left. They had piled everything they owned and what they'd stolen from the Tatums into their old car and gone. Callie's daddy sent one of the boys back to the house with the news. He whispered it to her mama, who didn't tell Callie until after she'd sent him off in the truck to call the sheriff. She gave Callie two aspirin tablets and put her to bed.

The Kellys were stopped on a downtown street in Deer Creek when the engine of their car caught on fire. Sam Kelly didn't have a driver's license or ownership papers to the car, and the policeman who investigated the traffic tie-up spotted the gun as being stolen. Russell had burned his own name onto the walnut stock in fancy, swirling letters right after he got it. Before sundown of the same day that he killed Russell, Sam Kelly was locked up in the county jail.

People brought food to the house like it was a church

dinner-on-the-ground Sunday. Callie stayed in the bedroom with the door shut, away from the bustle her mama's
friends made in the front part of the house. Two days later
they buried Russell from the Baptist Church. Her daddy
said it was the first time he had ever been to a funeral where
the body didn't lie in state beforehand. The undertaker
admitted he couldn't patch Russell up well enough to have
an open casket. Her mama said Callie should not view him
at all, but she didn't have to; she knew what he looked like
dead. She could see in her mind the exact place on his
forehead where the blast from the shotgun entered; she
could see his brains spewed in a puddle on the plank floor
of the porch where he fell. Arletta had sent Rafe to clean up
the place after the people from the funeral home took
Russell's body away.

Russell was buried in the dark blue suit he was married
in. Callie took it from the closet, and it smelled of moth
balls and of him; it felt like something alive in her hands.

Russell's daddy was more paralyzed than before and
couldn't, or wouldn't, talk at all. Lela went to pieces over
her brother's death, wailing at the funeral and also over the
fact that she was the only one in their family left to take care
of her daddy. On the day of Russell's death, after someone
fetched Lela to the farm in a state of shock over what had
happened, Callie tried to console her. She told Lela that
she would be glad to have Mr. Will stay on there with her
and Lucy. Callie's daddy reminded her then that she would
be the one leaving. The farm wasn't going to be Callie's,
since it had never been her husband's. The farm belonged
to Mr. Will. Her daddy thought that as soon as possible
she'd best gather up her things and move, with her baby,
on back "home."

"But what will happen to Mr. Will?" she asked him, not
where Lela could hear.

"Well, it's not for you to say," he said. "Likely as not Lela and her husband will move in and take care of him. When he dies, and he sure don't look long for this world, what would have been Russell's half of the property ought, by rights, to go to you as his widow and then to his little girl. I'll look into that right away." He cleared his throat with purpose.

Callie liked the thought of her daddy looking into something again. Her mama had pretty much taken charge of his dairy farming operation, keeping up with which cows were producing and how much, the amount sold and the amount that spoiled, writing it all down on lined tablets. Her daddy said, "They always say hindsight is better than foresight, but it would sure have been a fine thing if you had talked Russell into buying that life insurance."

"What life insurance?" Callie didn't catch the drift of what he was saying.

"Why, whatever that man from Birmingham was trying to sell you."

Everybody seemed to know there was a man from Birmingham.

13

She didn't tell Mr. Will she was leaving. He didn't appear to understand anything anyway. The vacant look that used to come in his eyes some of the time was now there all the time. She wanted to believe that he didn't know that Russell was dead and she was the cause of it.

Lela stood in the doorway, watching as Callie packed up, probably making sure she didn't take anything that wasn't hers. "My brothers will be over later today to get my bed and hope chest," Callie said.

"Good. It'll be a lot simpler to have your stuff cleared out before we move ours in."

Callie had her arms full as she moved past Lela. "Well, goodbye," she said. She was saying farewell to the family she had married into; Lela was the only one left to hear it.

She was halfway down the front steps when Lela called out to her. "Take care, Callie. Lots of girls would have given their eye teeth to be married to Russell. I never thought you appreciated what a good deal you had, but believe me, I feel sorry for you now." She turned and went back inside the house, clicking the screen door firmly shut behind her.

Callie piled her things in the back of her mama's truck and was cranking up when she saw Clifford's car parked at the edge of the road near the mailbox. She pulled alongside. Her heart was as thick as a block of wood. The only feeling she had was one of disbelief. In a way, it was as though she had caused Clifton's death, too; how could he be alive, in the flesh?

Clifton got out of his car. He said, "I needed a look at you. It's been a long time." His face was dazzling in the sunlight. He was there, solid, of a piece. It was Russell who was forever scattered in fragments of remembering.

"Did you know about my husband?" she asked.

"What about him?" Nothing registered on his face but his pleasure in seeing her.

Callie said, "I can't tell you here. Will you follow me in your car up the highway a piece?" She drove off first and led the way to a place where they both could pull off the road behind some trees. She got out of the truck and into his car, sitting as close to the door as she could. She told him what had happened as if it were a lesson she had memorized for school. His face turned white and he looked as if he might faint when she explained that it began with what Sam Kelly did to her, but he didn't interrupt.

After she finished, they sat in silence for at least a minute. Then Clifton said, "I never saw anything about it in the Birmingham newspapers. Usually, a killing like that, with rape involved, would be headline news." He hesitated over the word "rape." Callie knew he was embarrassed and didn't know what to say to her about it. He shuddered and wiped his face with his handkerchief. Then he did what she hadn't been able to do; he blamed it on Russell. "Your husband should never have let a man like that live on the place." He hadn't made a move to touch her.

"I've been living with my folks since it happened," Callie said. "I had gone back over there just now to get up some of my things." She opened the car door, got out, and started to breathe normally again. While she was in his car, she was having a hard time not throwing herself on him, just to feel the reality of him. "I'm glad you came so I could tell you. I figured you didn't know anything about it." Actually, she figured he was dead, too, to her.

"Wait. Don't go yet. I'm still reacting to this. I don't mean to sound unsympathetic about what you have suffered. But you do see what this is for you and me, don't you, Callie?"

"God's punishment?"

"You think God's punishment would be to have you raped and your husband gunned down by a monster like that Kelly?"

"I don't know," she said. "I was wondering if that's what you think."

"Then no, that's not what I think." He sighed and said, with less exasperation, "Look. It's a terrible coincidence, the fact that your husband was murdered soon after my wife committed suicide. But you and I have been set free by these events we had no control over, that we didn't cause to happen." The color came back into his face as he talked. "After that man's trial is past, and things have settled down here for you, I can come and call on you publicly. We can hold our heads up, because we are completely innocent. Don't you see?"

"Not really," Callie said. "I don't feel innocent about what happened to your wife or to my husband. I feel like we turned on the gas stove and aimed the shotgun, as though we planned their deaths and carried them out together."

Anger lit his face like a candle. "That's the most ridiculous thing I ever heard of."

"Anyway, why would you want me, after Sam Kelly—"

"I won't let myself think about that. I hardly remember what he looks like, after the one brief encounter I had with him. Now I don't ever want to see him again; therefore, I won't attend his trial. Do you think you'll be put on the stand?"

"I don't know. My folks don't want to have to acknowledge the rape publicly any more than necessary, so we're not pressing that charge. But I don't want you to come. Something bad might get said about me in that courtroom."

For the first time, he seemed wary; he looked at her like Lela had. "What could get said about you other than the fact that you were a victim?"

"Nothing. I don't know why I said that." She was back inside the truck with the door closed. They were talking through the open windows.

"Callie," Clifton said slowly, "I don't think I would have had the nerve to defend your honor and go after that man like your husband did. I'm not very brave."

"I'm sure I wouldn't have had the nerve to do what your wife did, either," she said. "I would never have put myself out of the way, in order to free you for another woman."

She had meant to return the compliment, but "That wasn't why she did it," he snapped. "Mary was mentally unbalanced. Finding your letter just caused her to go ahead with the suicide she'd been contemplating for years anyway."

They had driven away in opposite directions before the heavy yearning to touch him let her go, like a kite let loose from its string.

∽

The date of the trial came before the ground had settled over Russell's grave, which was still unmarked. Lela had insisted on ordering the tombstone herself, since, as she put it, "My daddy's money will pay for it." The block of marble would come from the deep quarry a few miles away. Callie had asked Lela what inscription she intended to have carved on it, but Lela told her to wait and see. Callie assumed it would be something that sounded like scripture but wasn't, like on Russell's mother's tombstone: "She trusted in the Lord with all her soul." Russell hadn't trusted in anyone, not even the Lord. He'd figured he had to look out for himself. He might still be alive except that he forgot about looking out for himself and thought only of avenging the damage done to her.

Each day, she took whatever flowers were blooming in her mama's garden—tea roses, or a handful of daisies—and left them, in a five-and-ten-cent store vase, at the head of his grave where the marker would be placed. After the vase disappeared, she left flowers in a Ball jar with a nicked place on the rim. A chipped jar wasn't safe for canning, so maybe no one would take it.

Everybody thought the killer was sure to get the electric chair. A buzz of surprise filled the courtroom when the judge pronounced the sentence of life imprisonment. But the real gasps in the courtroom had come earlier, when Callie took the stand and Sam Kelly's court-appointed lawyer asked her that terrible question. "Mrs. Tatum, isn't it a known fact that you were in the habit of granting certain favors to men who visited the Tatum farm when you husband was away at his job in town?" He emphasized the word in such a way that no one could miss what kind of favors he meant.

The county prosecutor jumped up and shouted "I object to this line of questioning, your honor!" and the judge sustained it, but the point was made. Practically everybody in the courtroom had known Callie since she was born. She could see all those pairs of eyes reflecting a single opinion of her.

Fuel was added to the flame when Evie Kelly gave her testimony, looking even more pitiful than Callie remembered her, in her advanced state of pregnancy in a feed sack dress that hadn't even been ironed. The lawyer asked Evie why her husband had gone to see Mrs. Tatum on that fateful morning. She answered as though she didn't understand the question: "All Sam done to her was what those others had been doing. Callie Tatum had a steady stream of men coming around there while her husband was working his mill shift. I seen them going in and out of that house up the hill just about every day." She didn't avoid looking at Callie while she said that. She stared straight at her. Callie could see the woman thought she was telling the truth. The prosecutor objected again, and the judge told Sam Kelly's lawyer to stick to the crime being tried, and not lead the witness down other avenues.

Her mama, sitting beside Callie on the front row, spoke up as though she had a right to enter the proceedings. "Well, my stars, white trash will lie as easy as they kill and plunder, won't they?"

Her daddy rubbed his forehead with his hand, trying to keep his eyes covered. Her brothers were redder than bad sunburn, they were so embarrassed. Arletta and Rafe were in the back of the courtroom, the only colored people in there. They stood near the door, and when Callie and her folks left after the trial was over, Arletta beamed her a message. She was sending Callie her own strength to help her get down that aisle, out that door, and back into her own private self. It was as clear to Callie as if she had shouted words of encouragement, in Arletta's fierce smile and the defiant tilt of her chin.

Callie smiled back at Arletta and raised her own chin,

and at that moment a man with a big black camera, waiting outside the door, snapped her picture. Later, someone brought her daddy a copy of the Birmingham newspaper that had a photograph of Callie emerging from that court-room, grinning as though she didn't care what people thought of her. The article that ran with it stated, "Mrs. Tatum was reputed to have many men attracted to her, and such speculation may have triggered her husband's wrath and jealousy." She could not bear to imagine what Clifton thought as he read those words. Because he surely would have seen her picture and read all about Sam Kelly's trial in his hometown newspaper.

After they had left the courthouse and were driving home, her daddy cleared his throat and announced to Callie, her mama, and her brothers, that they were not going to re-hash the trial. "Justice has pretty much been done," he said. "Most men would rather die in the electric chair than have to spend the rest of their lives in a rat-infested hole like Kilby Prison." Callie's brothers wanted to argue that point. She knew they were just big talking when they said they wanted to get up a group and take Sam Kelly out of the law's custody and lynch him. Callie's mama jumped in and said "Y'all will do no such thing. We're a law-abiding family." She added, "That wife of his screamed like a Holy Roller at a tent revival when the judge pro-nounced sentence. What did she expect, anyway?"

Callie's daddy repeated solemnly, as though he were a judge, "I said we will not have any more discussion on this sorry business."

Callie was wedged in front between him and her mama. She felt like she was on an island of safety. She looked out the window and saw Russell's murderer in the clouds with a noose around his neck. The hanging rope was looped over a branch of the tree that Mr. Will sat under to survey his land. She closed her eyes to firm up the vision. She'd rather see Sam Kelly swinging there dead than panting like a wild beast, as he did when he violated her, or whining like a whipped cur dog as he had during his trial. She had thought she would feel something definite, like pleasure at seeing justice done, or anger and disappointment that it was only partially done. But inside her was only a cool bleak emptiness. She hoped that meant she had already stopped using up her life's energy on hating Sam Kelly.

It was as though she had come home from a trip somewhere far off as she settled back in her old room in the house where she'd grown up. The bulletin board with the dried gardenia corsage from her senior prom, the only flowers Russell had ever given her, still hung on one wall. Wiping the light film of dust off her dresser was like wiping away her absence, the two years and almost three months of her marriage.

She had taken Lucy back to see Mr. Will a few days after the funeral, but he didn't give any sign of recognition, and Lucy fussed when she tried to put her down on the bed beside him. It was clear to Callie that Lela no longer regarded her as an in-law relative. But Callie's daddy did persuade Lela to let Callie have the car. He had tried to get Russell's truck for her, too, explaining to Lela that the truck could be sold and the money would be used to help raise her brother's child; didn't she feel any compassion for little Lucy? Lela's answer was that her own daddy's money had paid for the truck in the first place, and it would be needed on the farm. "Seems to me Callie could go to work, taking in sewing," she said.

Lela had given her an idea, after all. Without even asking her mama's opinion, Callie went to see Mrs.

Compton. She waited in the darkened gloom of the store until a customer had left. Then, trying to sound cheerful, she called out, "Afternoon, Mrs. Compton."

Mrs. Compton returned the greeting, adding, "I heard about your husband, and what all you've gone through." She kept going without a pause: "I hear Will Tatum had another stroke and won't come out of this one."

"That's what the doctor says," Callie said, thinking, your lost love is really lost to you now; what you and he shared is locked away in his paralyzed brain.

Mrs. Compton's eyes narrowed as though she read Callie's mind. "Can I help you?"

"I hope so. I need to make a living now, for me and my little girl. My plan is to find some ladies to sew for. I was wondering—" She hesitated, then plunged on quickly, "If you would let me put an Alterations and Dressmaking sign in your store, with my name and my folks' phone number."

Mrs. Compton looked as though Callie had asked her for a loan. "You mean you want to set up your sewing machine in here? I don't have space for anything like that."

"Oh, no, ma'am. I just wanted to let your customers know where to get their sewing needs taken care of, with a sign that wouldn't take up much room, maybe by the cash register..."

"You wouldn't get any business from a sign in this place," Mrs. Compton said. "Nobody with a halfway decent car or truck stops here anymore. We hardly ever sell any gasoline; don't know why we keep a pump. We get mostly nigras, in wagons or on foot. Everybody else goes into town, where the selection is better and the prices cheaper, or so they think 'til they get there. You yourself go to Hill's; I understand that, because they give you more for your eggs than I could. That's beside the point, though. What you ought to do is go to one of those dress shops in

Clearwater or Deer Creek, see if you can't strike a deal to do their alterations free in exchange for a place to pick up some customers for your own sewing."

"That's a wonderful idea," Callie said. She had noticed, as Mrs. Compton talked, that the woman had pretty, even white teeth. Callie could see what she must have looked like when Mr. Will was attracted to her. "I'm going to do that very thing," she added. "I'll try in Clearwater first, since it's closer."

She got a sack of sugar from a nearby shelf, and took her coin purse from her dress pocket. She wanted to buy something, and sugar would keep until it was needed.

Mrs. Compton reached inside a large glass jar by the cash register. "Take this Guess What to your little girl," she said, handing her a waxed paper wrapper, twisted at the ends, that held chewy candy and a surprise, such as a wax whistle or a tiny celluloid doll. "Be sure she doesn't put the surprise in her mouth."

"Yes ma'am," Callie said, taking the offering, "Thank you. She'll love it." That Guess What might have been the first thing Mrs. Compton had given free to anyone since she gave her love to a man who wasn't her husband.

14

The Lady Louise Dress Shop was on Main Street between the drugstore and the barber shop. The mannequin in the display window had a painted-on face and hair. One of her hands was missing, but Miss Larson, the owner, always positioned that arm so that it didn't show from the street. Callie opened the door, setting off a little bell that sounded like a lady laughing. There wasn't much floor space inside between the two long boxed-in racks of dresses. Miss Larson wiggled her feet back into her high heeled patent leather pumps, put her magazine down and got up from a straight chair.

Callie hated to disappoint the lady by making her think she had a customer. She had memorized what she had to say, but she was so nervous her voice wobbled as she said her name: "I'm Callie Tatum. I could do alterations for you, free, in exchange for a place to collect some sewing work to do at home." She had got it all out in a piece; she breathed again.

"I know who you are, hon. You've been through a rough time, haven't you? Lost your husband and all. And so you need to work now?" Miss Larson wore her bright hennaed hair in precise finger-waves, even though the style in the magazines had changed to a looser look. Her fingernails were painted a soft rose, with oval white tips and half moons at the base of each nail left plain. Callie

knew the story about Miss Larson. She had been engaged
to a soldier who was killed in the World War. He was
supposed to be buried across the ocean, in a place called
Flanders Field. Miss Larson still wore the engagement ring
he'd given her on her left hand. At least it kept people from
thinking of her as an old maid. Another story was that a
man from Mississippi came once a month to spend a
weekend with her. She told people he was her cousin, but
Callie's mama said she didn't believe it for a minute; he
probably had a wife and children at home.

Miss Larson was busy looking at Callie's dress, the one
she'd worn the time Clifton took her to the Gladjoy Hotel.
The neckline had a soft bias ruffle and the skirt was cut on
the bias, too, so that it floated when she walked. "Where'd
you get that pretty frock?" Miss Larson asked her.

"I made it. I started out with a Simplicity pattern, but I
changed it some. I was copying a picture of a dress Joan
Bennett had on in *Motion Picture Magazine*."

"Do you think you could copy a picture of a dress
without a pattern?"

She hadn't had time to make herself that many clothes,
which was the only way she could experiment. Now that
she had no house to run, no husband to cook for, no life to
live, she had the time. Callie said, "I believe I could."

"Well, I declare. You're too good just to do alterations.
Why don't we set you up in the back of my shop—you can
use the second dressing room, the one with a window, for
your sewing machine. Times aren't so good that I need to
reserve both these rooms for customers to try on ready-
mades." Miss Larson motioned for Callie to follow her. She
pulled a curtain aside from the opening to a small room.
"This is where you'll be. Here's how we'll start. You make
up a couple of dresses in size ten, and get material that
looks real nice, but isn't too expensive. My most popular

line is Nelly Don house dresses, because they're comfortable and fit women who've lost their shape, and they're
cheap. But I wouldn't mind something a little fancier."

"Batiste and voile, instead of chambray?" Callie suggested.

"Exactly," Miss Larson nodded. "Chambray is good,
close-woven cloth, but it seems ordinary because it's made
locally and everybody's used to it. Red is the color that sells
best. I don't know why, because not many women look
good in red. And pink is always popular too. You can
charge your time in making them at twenty-five cents an
hour. Add that to the cost of the material, thread, pattern,
and buttons. You ever put in a zipper?"

"I've just used buttons and snaps," Callie admitted. The
local dry goods store didn't have zippers in the notions
section. She could probably order some from Sears Roebuck.

"We'll double the total cost to come up with the price of
the dress, and split the profit fifty-fifty. Sound all right to
you?"

"Yes ma'am. That sounds fine." She was dizzy, trying to
keep up with Miss Larson's plans. But who would buy the
dresses?

Miss Larson answered her unspoken question. "We'll
display them prominently. I'll put Sadie, my window
dummy, in one dress. And the other can be draped over
the hall tree in the front there. And, since you'll be here
waiting to see if anyone's going to buy your dresses, you
might as well do my alterations. I haven't had anyone since
Mary Lou Higgins quit after she hurt her back. You can
charge the customers. I don't have to offer free alterations,
because my prices are reasonable enough as it is. Most will
just take up or let down their own hems, though, rather
than pay to have it done."

"Yes ma'am," Callie said again, overwhelmed. She actually had work; she would earn money.

"You wouldn't mind lending me a hand selling, too, would you? Sometimes a whole day will go by and not over one person will come in, but I have to be here. If you're in the shop, I could at least go across the street for a sandwich." Miss Larson smiled at Callie like she was the answer to a prayer.

Clifton had once told her she was the answer to a prayer he didn't know he prayed. Go away, she said in her mind, as his face filled up the space there.

⁓

Arletta came by her mama's house to see her on Saturday, the day after she'd been to talk to Miss Larson. Callie hugged her. "Arletta, I've sure missed you. How is it, now that you're working for Lela?

"Not as bad as I thought it would be. Rafe and Willie are both back working on the farm full time now. Miss Lela's husband don't know nothing about farming. He's even scared of the mules. She don't do nothing except wring her hands. She say she hate living out in the country again. But she's being extra nice to me. In fact, she want me and Rafe to move in that little house."

"Are you going to?" The idea of Arletta and Rafe living in the little house might help dispel the clear vision she had of Russell, lying sprawled across the doorway with his head blown apart, or the one she had of Clifton, standing in the open doorway, lit by a golden light, come for the stretched-out love that could make a lifetime of an hour.

Arletta's face showed she knew what line of thinking Callie was into. "No'm," she said softly. "I ain't interested in moving in there. Too much done gone on in that place.

I'd feel the shadows closing round me." She was standing, leaning on a wooden post at the edge of the front porch. Callie sat in a rocker, hand-basting the rolled hem of a dress for The Lady Louise.

"Look like you done caught a butterfly on your flypaper," Arletta said. The spiral of sticky paper, dotted with bodies of houseflies, hung from a ceiling hook by the front door. Also stuck there by the edge of one wing was a quivering black and yellow butterfly. Arletta reached up and gently extricated the creature. She placed it on the porch railing. "Her wing's not torn, but she probably won't try to fly, 'cause she thinks she can't."

Callie said, "Poor thing shouldn't have got trapped there in the first place. My mama's crazy on the subject of flies. She keeps swatters in every room, in case one of them does outwit her and get inside, and you ought to see how she is about mosquitoes. Come five o'clock every afternoon, she gets out the Flit gun and sprays everywhere. Arletta, do sit down," Callie said. Her mama would die, but she wasn't there. She had taken Lucy off with her to do some errands.

But Arletta didn't sit in one of the large oak rockers. She perched on the railing near the butterfly and fanned herself with a pasteboard paddle that had a picture of Jesus on one side and advertising slogans on the other. Jesus's face swayed back and forth as Arletta said, "Where you going to church now, Miss Callie?"

"Nowhere. I never got used to being a Baptist, and I won't go back to the Methodist with my folks."

"Does your mama know what that preacher tried to do?"

"I sure haven't told her. She doesn't want to know anything like that." Callie bit off a piece of thread and aimed it through the needle's eye. "At least she hasn't asked the preacher and his wife to Sunday dinner since I've been here."

Arletta lowered her voice and her gaze. She knew she was stepping out of line to ask the question. "What about that man from Birmingham, Miss Callie?"

"That's over and done with." She was trying to mean that.

"He still with his wife, then?"

Just as she thought, Rafe had looked inside the wallet that day and found the pictures of Clifton's wife. That's the only way Arletta could have known the man was married. "His wife died," Callie said.

"Did she die before or after Mr. Russell got killed?" Arletta kept her voice as casual as Callie's.

"Not long before."

"That kind of coincidence is too strange. Have to be the work of something or someone. You believe in Satan, Miss Callie?"

Callie sighed. "Doesn't everybody?" Her mama's black Bible with the gold-edged pages had a picture of the devil with pointed ears, hooves for feet, and a tail shaped like a pitchfork.

"Old Satan's behind that kind of coincidence," Arletta murmured so low that Callie thought if she asked her to repeat what she'd said, she wouldn't say the same words again.

"I got to get home before the sun goes all the way down, else I'll see Satan behind every tree. Shouldn't have brought up his name," Arletta said. Soon after she left, the black and yellow butterfly rose gracefully from the porch railing and soared skyward. Callie wished Arletta had stayed long enough to see it.

∽

She was settled into her new routine. She spent most of her long weekdays in the dress shop's small back room, lulled by the competing noises of her sewing machine and the floor fan. From time to time Miss Larson would sing out to her from the long narrow salesroom, "Oh, Callie—come on out here, hon. Mrs. Steagall's here to talk to you about a new outfit." She never said "dress," it was always "outfit."

Miss Larson had not mentioned Callie's troubles to her since that first time. But Callie knew she was still a topic of conversation in Clearwater, maybe Deer Creek, too. Sometimes she went to the drugstore and got a milkshake or a chocolate soda for her lunch. A rumble of talk would come to a sudden halt as she took a seat on a tall stool at the marble counter. Some might nod at her, but no one came over and sat by her or started a conversation. Not even the ladies she sewed for had anything to say to her when they saw her away from the dress shop. One day, Callie thought, it will be like nothing happened: I will come in and no one will turn and stare and then look away quickly. No talk will stop.

She asked her mama, "Do you think folks will ever be able to see me and not think of Russell and how he died?"

Her mama said, after a moment's consideration, "Frankly, I doubt it. But no matter what they think, you just have to hold your head up and act as though nothing has happened."

"How can I? Terrible things have happened."

"I know, and you'll never forget any of it, but you have to rise above it." Her mama didn't look her full in the eye like she used to.

Callie took hand-sewing home to do after her full days at the dress shop. She wanted to stay busy from the time she got up in the morning until she went to bed at night, as she'd been brought up to do, but her family treated her like a guest in the house. Her mama wouldn't let her help with the washing, ironing, and cooking. Lucy was thriving under the attention of her grandparents and uncles. She no longer said "Dad-dee" when she heard a truck drive up.

Callie got where she could sleep in the middle of the bed again. At first, she stayed on one side, as though the other side still belonged to Russell. At first, she would wake in the night and think she could feel his presence there beside her, hear the tiredness rise from his bones in the sounds of his breathing, before the emptiness of that space loomed up scarier than the thought of what she knew could not be.

Then she got to where she could wake in the morning knowing, before she opened her eyes, that she was alone, with a full day to face, and him not coming in at the end of it: The orange and purple sunset was as still as a calendar picture on the wall, because Russell did not roll to a brake-screeching halt in front of it; did not slam the door of his truck and whistle his way across the yard, up the back steps and into the house.

Clifton called her at her mama's. She answered, with the premonition she used to get that he would be on the other end, but it was spookier hearing his voice than the dreams she'd had about Russell. She jumped when he said her name.

"Callie." She really couldn't speak. "Callie," he said again, "Is that you?"

"Yes," she said then. "How are you?"

"I'm all right. How are you? I know you've been through hell. I had to give you time to get through the worst of it. That's why I stayed away."

"Oh," she said, trying to make some sense of that explanation. "Well, I just take one day at a time." That was the advice the Baptist preacher had given her right after the funeral, and what most well-meaning folks had said when they came to call, before the trial, before they saw her in a different light.

"I'm coming to see you tomorrow. Do you want to meet me somewhere, or should I come out to your folks' place?"

She couldn't let him do that; she didn't know how to explain him. But she wanted to see him. It was as if the sound of his voice filled her veins, as if her life's blood had been drained for weeks, and was now replenished.

She said, "Maybe we could meet again in the park in Clearwater. Not to go to the tourist cabin, I didn't mean meet like that." But she did mean meet like that.

His voice was smooth with a serenity she didn't understand how he could feel: "Ah, Callie. We don't have to hide anymore. Everything will be in the open from now on. But of course we can't make love in the open, so that part will just have to wait until we're married. I want you to bring Lucy with you to the park tomorrow."

For the rest of the day, she was scared and giddy, almost light-headed. It reminded her of the way she felt just before she got baptized in the holy green waters.

She explained to Miss Larson that something had come up and she couldn't be at work the next morning. She didn't explain anything to her mama except that she would be taking Lucy into town with her.

Lucy, scrubbed with Ivory soap until she gleamed, in a pink and white checked gingham frock with a white eyelet pinafore, a ribbon tied around her head, stood next to her in the front seat. Callie had on one of the flower print dresses she'd made for the store but decided to keep for herself.

She saw him as soon as she drove into the park. He was standing near the bandstand with two children who weren't tiny, like Lucy. They looked half like their daddy, and half, she supposed, like their mother; and they looked at her with fear and distrust written all over their tight faces. Clifton made the introductions quickly, stumbling over the names in his eagerness. He smiled anxiously as he looked from his children to Callie. He told them she was his "new friend." He pretended he didn't see how miserable she and his children were. Callie shifted Lucy from one arm to the other.

"Would you let Susan take Lucy over to the swing set?" Clifton didn't wait for an answer. He took the baby from her and put her down. The girl reached for Lucy's hand. Callie watched them head toward the swings. After a minute of embarrassed immobility, the boy ran after them.

"She'll be fine. Susan is a very responsible girl for her age. She's going to love having a little sister." Clifton led Callie to a bench, and they sat down slowly, like two old people unsure of whether the bench would hold their combined weight, and carefully not too close together.

"Your children are attractive," Callie said. The boy had on a sailor suit and knee-socks. The girl wore a dotted swiss dress that was wrinkled from the long car ride. Her hair was braided in neat pigtails with the ribbons evenly tied. Someone had been looking after them. They didn't look like half-orphans.

"They won't give you any trouble. They've been in the care of their strict grandmothers, and they'll be happy to be back home again." Clifton gazed at his children with pride.

"You mean they've actually been living with your mother and your wife's mother? Not with you?"

"Well, I have them part of the time," he said. "The arrangement has worked out well so far. But the children need to be in a normal home situation again, with both a mother and a father."

"It wouldn't be normal. Every time they looked at me, they'd wish for their own mother." She felt the urge to clarify details, as the lawyers had in the courtroom. Until then, she'd thought it was always better to avoid argument. She was about to add that Lucy wouldn't be Susan's little sister, either, but Clifton interrupted.

"They've accepted the fact that their mother has passed away," he said. "And they will accept the fact that their father needs another wife now, someone who will be a new mother to them. We'll take it a day at a time."

It was like they were already married. They were sitting on a bench in a public park, watching their children play; they were not touching each other, not dying to touch each other. "We can't," she said.

"Can't what?"

"Can't marry each other." She wanted to grab Lucy and run, but that urge to explain held her rooted. "Not after what we did."

"We didn't do anything!" He really was puzzled. "You were willing to go through with the ordeal of two divorces, but now that fate has stepped in and fixed things so that we could be together—"

Fate, or what Arletta called the devil.

He had stopped to take a breath. He rushed on: "We got our freedom by accident. We didn't do anything to cause it!"

She heard the word as though she'd been searching for it. "I need to get used to freedom, to know what it is for me, before I give it up again."

"Callie, be sensible. What you need is a husband to take care of you, to provide you with a home and hearth." He reached for her hand. "I've never stopped thinking about you, even though I wasn't with you during that man's trial. You haven't held that against me, have you?"

"No," she said. "As it turned out, I was on trial then, too, for being unfaithful to my husband." But he hadn't been accused publicly of being unfaithful to his wife.

He took a package of Lucky Strikes and a Ronson lighter from his shirt pocket. She watched him peel the thin red strip of cellophane, open the package and shake a cigarette from the tinfoil liner. He lit it and took a deep drag before he spoke again. "People where I live don't know anything about all that. Even if they read about it in the paper, they won't remember your name as being connected with that mess. There hasn't been a whiff of scandal about me with another woman, so they wouldn't see you as a homebreaker." He glanced at her briefly, as though to reassure himself she didn't look like a homebreaker. "If you're being given a hard time by people around here, then you really do need to get away and start over somewhere else."

He was right about that.

He threw the cigarette down and stepped on it. "Let's decide exactly what we're going to tell your folks and mine about how we met and got to know each other. Then, we'll just get married quietly. We'll go to a justice of the peace."

"Have you told your children about me?"

"No. I wanted them to meet you before they learn that you're going to be a part of their lives."

"That would be another shock for them."

"It won't be near like the shock of losing their mother. You and I are going to do what's right for us. Everything and everyone else will just have to fall in place." Clifton stood, looming over her like a sudden storm cloud. He was jiggling his keys in his pocket, anxious to get going, to be about the business of his life. It was like he had braked his car just long enough for her to hop on the running board.

She stood, and moved out of his shadow. In the near

distance, his daughter held Lucy on a seesaw; his son was kicking rocks quietly by himself.

She wanted to take Clifton's face in her hands, trace the shape of his mouth with her fingers. That's all she was thinking about: the shape of his mouth. She heard her next words with sorrow, a revelation to herself as well as to him. "I can't do it now," she said.

His shoulders hunched as though to ward off a blow. He reminded her of Russell, then. And of her daddy and Mr. Will. "So I'm supposed to raise my kids in a motherless home and wait for you to get over your guilt feelings or whatever it is that's got you hung up?" Clifton seemed more bewildered than angry.

"I guess you have to do whatever feels right for you," she said. She made herself stop looking at his mouth. She went over and got Lucy, who didn't want to be gotten. The children smiled at her, as Lucy begged to be put back down with them, but the fear was still on their faces. They probably would be easy to get close to, but she didn't have any extra love at the time to spill over on them. She only had enough for Lucy and herself. Clifton was there, flesh and blood, and she might have melted right into him if they had been by themselves, but even then, some part of her would have held back, and watched, and judged.

They parted that day with a handshake. It didn't seem odd at all at the time.

15

Her mama was waiting for her with questions. "Who was that man you were talking to in the park? The one with the children?"

Callie countered with one of her own. "Who told you anything about it?"

"Lela had the phone reconnected over there right after she moved in. She wouldn't say where she heard it, but she called me to ask all about him. Imagine how I felt, not knowing anything about any man with children, and having to admit as much to her."

"He's from out of town," Callie said.

"Well, I figured that much." After Callie didn't elaborate, her mama continued, "I assume he is the man from Birmingham. The one who called you about insurance that time."

"The one I hardly knew," Callie said, not even sure it was a lie. "He was just passing through." He had passed through her life like a tornado.

"What about his wife?"

"He's a widower."

Her mama's face brightened considerably. "I see," she said, and she was certainly trying to. She cleared her throat. "I'd like for us not to beat around the bush here anymore, Callie. I suspected you had got yourself involved somehow with a man, although to what extent I don't ever care to know. But enough that you got yourself talked about—"

Callie said, "Don't tell me what you've heard about me."

Her mama gasped. Back talk was something she had never put up with from her children, and Callie could see she wasn't sure how to handle it from her, since she was grown. "Oh, well," her mama said, "As far as I'm concerned, that's water over the dam now. If he's a good man, and willing to make an honest woman of you—"

No one had been anywhere near them in the park to overhear the conversation. Callie said, "What he did was make a dishonest woman of me. Or rather, I made one of myself, with him."

"Now wait a minute, Sister. All this is far too strong." Her mama placed one hand on her chest like she might be having trouble breathing. "All I meant to point out is that you're lucky to have another man who wants to marry you. There's nothing sadder in this world than a woman who's lost her reputation, unless it's one who's lost her husband, and much to my own heartbreak my only daughter has lost both." She held her hand up, as if to ward off any protest Callie might make. When she saw Callie was going to let her have her say, she continued: "And, if he lives away from here, why, that may work out just fine. Folks in Birmingham wouldn't know about your scandal. It wouldn't be such a distance that you couldn't come back right often to see us. I wouldn't want Lucy to grow up too far away—" She looked like she might cry. Then she brightened again. "But what I want more than anything, is for you to have a second chance. You were such a good girl growing up."

"A second chance for what?" Callie was almost wishing that the conversation in the park had been between her mama and Clifton in the first place, and she could have stayed out of it.

"Another chance to be a good wife to somebody. And

to have more babies. I know you could be a fine step-mother, too. Lela said that the man's children were behaving nicely—"

"So it was Lela herself who spied on me." Again.

Her mama went on as though she hadn't been interrupted. "Now, I want you to bring this man home to meet your family. I won't ask him any questions about how you two got together. I will let him know that we are fully prepared to accept him. And don't worry about your daddy. I'll see he keeps quiet, too." Her mama could have been planning a church social instead of the rest of her daughter's life. "Of course it hasn't been long since Russell died, but under the circumstances I think we should go through with a quiet little wedding as soon as possible. Maybe in the Baptist Church, since you're still officially on the roll there. Unless you can choose to rise above that ridiculous rumor about the Methodist preacher being your—well, whatever—and marry in our church again."

Callie had Lucy in her lap. Lucy's thumb was in her mouth, and her eyes went from one to the other of them as though she could follow the talk. "Mama, do you really think I could just move into some other woman's house—with her furniture, her children, her husband—and take up right where she left off?"

"Why, of course you can. You can make it all yours. This man is offering you a chance to get your life back on a straight course, and you'd better take it." Her mama's face was as hard as peanut brittle.

Callie said, "I sent him away this afternoon for good."

"Sent him away!" Her mama put her hand over her heart again.

"Because I can't do it again. I can't shape my whole life around a man."

"No reason why you should have to," her daddy said,

gruffly. He had come in without making a sound, holding his dirt-caked rubber boots. "No reason, either, why you can't go on off to college now, like maybe you should have done when you finished high school. We could keep your young'un here until you get your certificate. Then you could find yourself a teaching job."

Her mama looked like someone had hit her. "Stars above, Callie's too old to go to college! She's a widow with a child!"

Her daddy said, "Damn it, woman, she's twenty years old, and that ain't too old to go to college."

"Who's gonna pay for it?" Her mama yelped like a dog that had been kicked.

"I'll see to that," her daddy said. "Anyway, Callie can stay right here with us and not go to college, if she wants to. It's her choice. She sure don't have to take up with some other man again until she's good and ready."

Callie had been listening to them like she was eaves-dropping outside a door, without feeling a bit of need to enter the conversation. She closed her eyes against quick tears when her daddy said those last words, which were the last of the discussion; her mama looked completely out of control for the only time Callie could remember.

She was busy with her hands and fingers, sewing a ward-robe of dresses that she copied from magazine pictures for the bank president's wife. She could take the scissors, and using a bought pattern only as a sizing guide, make up her own pattern from old newspapers. Her hands caressed the garments as they took shape, as she brought forth dresses that moved as easily as dancers from flat, lifeless lengths of cloth.

But the engrossing work did not stop the thoughts and

feelings from darting in and out of her mind like chimney swallows. Sometimes, without warning, she would remember something fleeting of the love that she and Clifton had made between them; a piece of longing thin as a veil of mosquito net would come over her, and then it would float on off just as quickly as it came. At such times she made herself remember how it was with Russell before Clifton came into her life; how it was when Russell touched her and warmed her and made her feel secure. She saw both their faces in her mind: Clifton's, pale and serious; Russell's, dark and hurt-looking. She could not recall their smiles. But she remembered that sometimes their eyes lit up at the sight of her.

Clifton called, finally, one afternoon when her mama was away. He said he'd called several times before, but every time someone else besides Callie had answered, so he had hung up immediately. She didn't believe that, but she didn't say so. The wire hummed above the silence. She couldn't think of anything at all to say to him, but she sensed he had something to say to her. And then he told her, straight out and as quickly as he could, that he was getting married to a cousin of his wife's, someone he'd known for years, who had never been married before.

"Are you happy?" Callie asked.

"I feel a great relief. Being without a wife, even for a short time, has been a very difficult thing for me. The children were already close to Sylvia, and the grandmothers approve of her."

She wished he hadn't said the woman's name; she didn't want to have to imagine a face to go with it. She said, "Clifton, I'm really happy for you." She told herself she would be.

"Callie." His voice sounded the way it used to. "You were right. For us to be married to each other would have spoiled what we had. But now that the issue is settled, we can love each other even better. I'll see to it that we never come close to being caught again. We can keep the magic intact, just being together every now and then for an hour or so like before, don't you see? We can keep it because it's free, with no strings attached. That was what made it so wonderful in the first place…" He was talking fast, as if to keep her from interrupting, but she held the phone in stunned silence. He hesitated, then said, "Please, Callie?"

She said, wearily, "Don't come looking for me again, Clifton." She hung up so carefully there was hardly a click.

∼

Lela called to tell her the new tombstone was in place. "It's beautiful, if I do say so myself. I wanted Brother to have something fine to mark his final resting place."

Callie went by the cemetery as soon as she got off from work. Russell's tombstone stood out from the older markers in its whiteness. His mother's, less than three years old, had already turned milky-gray. Lela had done a good thing; she'd kept it simple. Callie sank to her knees beside the square stone and traced the indentations of the block letters with one finger.

WILLIAM RUSSELL TATUM, JR.
1914–1938
A BELOVED MAN

"Russell, you were my beloved," she said. She waited for a sign of forgiveness from him: a quick flash of summer lightning, the bright surprise of a redbird, a sudden breeze. No such thing occurred. Russell had nurtured his hurts; he never had learned how to let them go. His forgiveness would be a long time coming, if it ever did.

∽

Arletta answered her knock on the door. "Miss Callie, sugar, how you doing," she said. "I heard you was leaving. I said to myself, I hope she comes over and sees us 'fore she goes." She stepped back and held the door open for Callie to enter. "In fact, I was going to see could I hitch myself a ride to your mama's place after I get off today, so I could tell you goodbye."

"I wouldn't leave without coming by here." Familiar odors of the old house assailed her, especially the slight decaying smell of Mr. Will, like pockets encrusted with shredded tobacco. He was laid out on the stiff horsehair couch as though he were dead. Callie gasped. "Is he—?"

"He all right. He open his eyes in a minute, maybe."

Arletta touched the old man's shoulder. "Look who's here, Mr. Will," she said.

"He still can't say anything?" Callie whispered, knowing the answer before Arletta shook her head. She had already forgotten how it was to be around him, to regard him as a fixture in her life. He hadn't moved or opened his eyes. The dark blue veins on his right hand, which lay across his heart, were as thick as baling twine. She sat beside him on the couch, took that hand and pressed it to her. What harm, he had said, would a quick feel do? The hand stayed inert against the softness of her breast. He opened one eye then, and before he closed it again she thought she saw a gleam of recognition.

Arletta said, "Miss Lela was headed for town, won't be back for awhile. She be sorry to miss you."

"I passed her on the road. I had already told her goodbye. She won't be sorry to miss me, but it was nice of you to say so." Callie had come to see Arletta and Mr. Will and the house, to reclaim any elusive memories that might be waiting there for her. Now that she'd seen Mr. Will, she wished she hadn't. She stood, and said to Arletta, "Tomorrow's the big day. I bought myself a ticket to Columbus, Georgia."

"How long it take you to get there?"

"It's a four hour train ride. My mama carries on like I'm crossing the ocean instead of the state line. My daddy's made arrangements for me to stay with his second cousin once removed, an unmarried lady who owns a boarding house." The arrangements had taken place over the telephone, with her daddy shouting because he wasn't used to talking long-distance. He said the woman was hard of hearing anyway. Her mama wanted to do the talking, but he said it was his right because the kinship was through his side of the family.

Arletta said admiringly, "I'm proud for you. It takes some gumption to move that far away."

Callie said, as though compelled to give a reason for her move, "I wanted a change of scenery." Not Birmingham, but a medium-sized city with buildings, streets, sidewalks, traffic lights, noise. She had lived in the quietness long enough. "Mama ruled out Montgomery because we don't have kinfolks there. I'll find a dress shop in Columbus to take sewing orders through." She could see the shop in her mind. And eventually, she would have a shop of her own; she could see that one, too.

"What about Lucy?"

"She'll stay here with my folks until I get settled. I'm sure my mama is hoping and praying I'll find myself another husband as soon as possible. She probably thinks that's my real purpose in leaving home."

"And is it?"

"Believe me, I don't plan to look for another husband any time soon."

Arletta nodded. "You're right to take your time. You know how to make a living for yourself, so you don't have to be in no kind of rush to take up with some man again."

"I wish I could make my mama understand, but I don't see any sense in even trying."

"No'm, ain't no point in trying to change your mama's way of thinking. She too set in her ways."

Callie had moved away from the couch and Mr. Will; she wouldn't even try to say goodbye to him. "Arletta, I'll never find anybody else to talk to like I do you. Why don't you come with me?" She meant it.

"You know I couldn't do that, sugar," Arletta said reprovingly. "From what I hear, Georgia ain't no better for colored folks than Alabama, and life in a big town, they say, is a heap worse on us than life in the country. Anyway, I wouldn't know how to live anywhere 'cept with Rafe, in our cabin in the Quarters. But I'll miss you, Miss Callie, and I sure wish you the best."

Callie moved into the warm hug of Arletta's open arms. At the door, she turned for one last look around the front room. The spotted wildcat that Mr. Will had shot on a hunt the night before he married (she'd heard it as an allegory: his wild youth was being put to rest) crouched, mounted and moth-eaten, in a glass cage just inside the doorway. Miss Ruth's stiff arrangements of dark, dusty peacock feathers filled the blue hobnail glass vases on the mantel. The upright piano, that hadn't been played since Russell's grandmother died, was dark and closed like a coffin against the far wall. The rosewood parlor chairs, with crocheted doilies resting on the velvet arms as lightly as ladies' hands, had been there for fifty years.

Callie thought, with amazement: I did not leave a mark of my own in this place. There is nothing here of me, unless sounds of my laughter and crying are trapped in the walls, along with Lucy's baby-cooing and Russell's whistling and tantrums.

She looked at Arletta as though to memorize her face. "Take care. I'll write you a postcard soon after I get to Columbus."

"Not the plain kind," Arletta said. "You be sure to send me one with a picture on it, you hear?"

∾

Lucy had a cinder in her eye and was crying when Callie had to hand her to her daddy and climb aboard the train. Her whole family had dressed up like it was Sunday to come to the depot to see her off. She had a suitcase of new clothes she'd made for herself, plus the ready-made dress Miss Larson had given her as a farewell gift, and enough money to last her several weeks. By that time she expected to be earning some again. Her sewing machine was crated up in the baggage car.

She took a seat by a window. As the train pulled out, her mama waved a handkerchief back and forth in the air, like a signal flag. The shrill blasts of the train whistle seemed to proclaim the fact that she was really on her way. Within seconds the town was behind, in the past. The tracks ran downward on a pine-wooded slope through the deepest part of the valley, then onto a trestle over the wide part of Hatchet Creek. Beyond its banks, uncultivated land gleamed with goldenrod that reached toward heaven as sure as church steeples. Next came the first open, flat fields. A few optimistic cotton pickers were out with shoulder-slung pick sacks and big baskets, trying to make up a load for the gin.

The train rumbled along as confidently as a marching hymn. The familiar countryside—not altogether tamed despite the disciplined farms, rigid churches, and the testimonials of cemeteries—flew by like pieces of dreams.

Arletta was right. She didn't have to be in any kind of rush. When she'd cleared the cobwebs from the corners of her heart, swept it clean as a farmhouse yard, then, maybe, she would be ready to love a man again.

ACKNOWLEDGMENTS

I am grateful to Randall Williams for his enthusiasm and creative vision. I thank Tom Fitzpatrick for his interest and helpful advice, and Tom Conner for finding answers to several questions about the times depicted. I appreciate the generosity of Jane and Forrest McConnell in sharing, for the dust jacket, their painting of an Alabama countryside. I also wish to express my appreciation to the Alabama Department of Archives and History for the convenient availability of old newspapers on microfilm.

For his constant encouragement, I am indebted to my husband, Thomas Oliver.

JULIA OLIVER

About the Author

Julia Oliver lives in Montgomery, Alabama. Her collection of short fiction, *Seventeen Times as High as the Moon*, was published by the Black Belt Press in 1993.

DATE DUE